PENGUIN BOOKS

SEVENTEEN AND DONE (YOU BET!)

Vibha Batra is a copywriter by profession and fiction writer by passion. Her literary pursuits took off when she translated her grandfather Late Shri Vishnu Kant Shastri's book on the Ishaavaasya Upanishad (Rupa & Co., 2007). Among her recent titles are *Sweet Sixteen (Yeah, right!)* published by Penguin, *Tongue in Cheek*, a collection of poetry, and *A Twist of Lime*, a collection of short stories.

To connect with Rinki and learn more about this book, visit www. seventeenanddone.facebook.com

W0050197

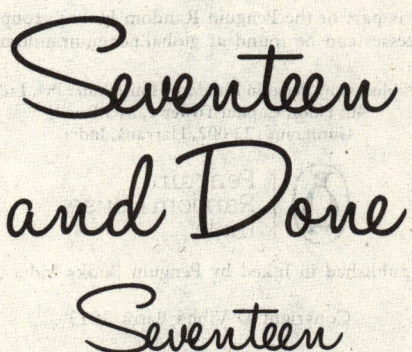

Seventeen and Done Seventeen

Vibha Batra

PENGUIN BOOKS

An imprint of Penguin Random House

PENGUIN BOOKS

USA | Canada | UK | Ireland | Australia
New Zealand | India | South Africa | China | Singapore

Penguin Books is part of the Penguin Random House group of companies
whose addresses can be found at global.penguinrandomhouse.com

Published by Penguin Random House India Pvt. Ltd
4th Floor, Capital Tower 1, MG Road,
Gurugram 122 002, Haryana, India

Penguin
Random House
India

First published in Inked by Penguin Books India 2013

Copyright © Vibha Batra 2013

All rights reserved

10 9 8 7 6 5 4 3 2

ISBN 9780143332947

Typeset in Perpetua by Eleven Arts, Delhi

Printed at Manipal Technologies Limited, India

This book is sold subject to the condition that it shall not, by way of trade
or otherwise, be lent, resold, hired out, or otherwise circulated without the
publisher's prior consent in any form of binding or cover other than that in
which it is published and without a similar condition including this condition
being imposed on the subsequent purchaser.

www.penguin.co.in

MIX
Paper | Supporting
responsible forestry
FSC® C043100

This is a legitimate digitally printed version of the book and therefore might not
have certain extra finishing on the cover.

For MRS^2

for JIPS

Acknowledgements

Huge thanks and much love to all the usual suspects: my Naani-Babuji, Mom-Dad, in-laws and extended family, my personal wolf pack (Mitu, Teels, Mones), my professional wolf pack (Sohini, Amrita and team), and of course, all my readers. And to the one who didn't (inadvertently, of course) make it to the last list: HP.

Prologue

Facebook Status Update: Rinki Tripathi joined the group 'I am from Chennai and that automatically makes me a hundred times cooler than you.'

So, I was wrong.

The summer of 2010 was NOT the worst summer of my life. Actually, as summers go, it was a Titanic (not the super hit movie, the ship). But then 2011 came along, and all of a sudden, 2010 didn't seem so bad after all.

I know what you're thinking:

1. Haven't we been through all this? Did we just hit the rewind button here? (Sadly, no. Can't say I blame you, though. This is one deadly déjà vu, all right!)
2. Boyfriend trouble again? (Flashback: Last year, I starred in this sorry love story with one Mr TJ. Let's just say, it didn't have a happy ending. À la Beyoncé, am so rooting for all the single ladies right now.)
3. Hair straightening job gone wrong? (Shudder, shudder! No. Knock on wood. I have just found the bestest parlour

1

in Chennai. Yay! Now if I can only find the finances for it . . . ☺)

So, why me cry? Why was Miss Rinks in Angstville?

Cut to May 2011. Final exams were over and done with. XI grade was over and done with. Most importantly, trip to Delhi was over and done with. I was actually looking forward to two weeks of doing . . . nothing, when, BAM! Dad summoned an EFM (Emergency Family Meet).

I don't know about you, but around these parts, an EFM means only one thing: Trouble. Biiiiiig run-for-dear-life trouble!

Allow me to explain.

An EFM is like a *brahmaastra* (divine weapon, very lethal) that can be called upon by the elders at the time of, what else—an emergency. Kind of like those 'intervention' thingies on one of my favourite sitcoms, *How I Met Your Mother*.

So there we were, huddling around the centre table. Had we been holding hands, I'm sure we'd have looked like one big, happy family. Had we been holding hands. But but but . . . Dad's hands were playing a neat tabla on the table. My hands were fiddling with the iPad. Mom's hands were in a big bowl of butter popcorn.

And then, Dad turned to look us square in the eye. At least, he looked me square in the eye. Mom's eyes were busy tracking the descent of a runaway popcorn.

'Ladies, I have to tell you something.'

My blood ran cold. That's exactly how he'd dropped the 'We're moving to Chennai' bomb on us last summer.

I held my breath.

'I've been transferred,' Dad whispered, right on cue.

Pin-drop silence in the room. Correction: we could only hear Mom's teeth chomping away merrily on the popcorns.

Could it really be? Could lightning strike the same place twice? I mean, what were the chances? We'd moved to Chennai only last year. And just about settled in. What could be worse than Chennai, I thought hysterically. Somalia? Ethiopia? One of those tiny African countries Brangelina loved adopting kids from?

I jumped to my feet. 'No, Dad. I refuse to become a pirate who kidnaps . . . .uh, hijacks . . . oh, does whatever it is they do to ships . . .'

'Ships? What ships? What on earth are you babbling about, Rinki?' Dad asked, bewildered.

'I'm not going, Dad. I'm not going anywhere,' I declared, stomping my feet.

'Wash aboush my sharee shaaaphs?'

That was Mom, her mouth full of popcorn.

'What?' Dad swung around to look at her.

'She means "what about my saree shops"?' I subtitled.

Great. Since when did I start speaking Popcornese?

'Ladies, ladies, ladies. Didn't you listen to a word of what I was saying? I said *I* was getting transferred.'

I narrowed my eyes. So did Mom.

'As in me, myself and I. I am going to Coimbatore for a project. Shouldn't take me more than a couple of months to wrap it up.'

Oh? Oh!

There was a moment of respectful silence. I could hear two brains working away furiously: Mom's and mine.

'You're going away for shiksh whole monthsch?' murmured Mom.

'And taking the iPad with you?' I said, without missing a beat.

'Whash aboush Rinki's school, her shudiesh?' Mom did it again.

'I wouldn't want to uproot Rinki,' Dad consoled.

Yeah, right.

'It's her Board year, after all.'

Like I needed any reminding.

Suddenly, without warning, hope sprang in my heart and floated up. Gosh, Dad *and* Mom would go away to Coimbatore. And while the cats were away, Rinki the Rat would be at play. Oooh, yeah! I'd be like Priyanka in *Dostana*. I'd get an all new wardrobe, two super hot (male) paying guests. Oh, not for me. To help Mom and Dad out with the rent, of course.

Ohmmmygooosh, I was so excited! I was totally going to rock. Life was finally going to look up for Rinki Tripathi. Yay! In the words of my favourite spy, Austin Powers, 'Groovy, baby!'

'Don't worry. To make things easier for you, I've asked Mausiji to come stay with you and Mom,' Dad consoled.

Crassssshhh!

Chill, that was not the sound of my heart breaking. It was the sound of Mom's popcorn bowl clattering to the floor.

'Whash? Howsh coulsh you do thisch to me?'

'What? How could you do this to me?' I translated like a zombie on auto mode.

Backstory: Mom had no 'lau' (as they say Down South) lost for Mausiji, Dad's aunt. In fact, if there was one person on earth my mom couldn't stand, it was her. Earlier, it used to be Daadi, Dad's Mum. And Mausiji was basically her evil twin. (Mom's words, not mine. My interaction with Dad's side of the family was pretty much like a Bollywood starlet's clothing and IQ. Tantalizingly brief and nothing to write home about).

Cut to the present.

Mom flew out of the room, Dad close on her heels. 'Come on, Sheena. Don't be cross,' he cajoled.

Well, well, well. Talk about a twist in the tale.

The sudden turn of events got me thinking. I mean, any of these three things could happen:

1. My life was not going to get affected at all. One jailer, two jailers, same difference.
2. My life would get a shade better. With Dad out of the way, I could actually stretch my deadlines (and ergo, my luck). Have a little fun in the last year of my life. (School life/ life, same thing).
3. My life would nosedive. Get worse than last summer. (Hah, not likely.)

I was still pondering over my future when Mom came out of her *kop bhawan* (sulking room—gosh, don't you ever read those epics?) and muttered, 'Rinki, where do you get the best Kanjivarams in Coimbatore?'

I dutifully reached for the iPad.

Google search: Silk saree stores in Coimbatore

Psst. To make matters worse, the family's backbone—our hired help—announced the same day that she was quitting. The news hit Mom wayyyy harder than Dad's transfer. I mean, she barely sniffed while waving Dad goodbye. But when the time came for Maheshwari's departure, she howled like a baby. Like she said, 'Your dad'll be back in six months but Maheshwari? How on earth will I find a maid as good as her?'

I didn't know the answer to *that* question. So I went to this uber-cool website exclusively for teenagers that posed easier ones. I always found it a great way to pass time. And ponder over life's big questions.

Rinki Tripathi is taking an online quiz on Teenz Forever.

Quiz Number #333. Chameleon or Dinosaur: What's your personality type?

1. Your friends ask you if you want to go bungee jumping. You:
    a. Jump to your feet and ask 'How soon can we leave?'
    b. You are scared but convince yourself *'Darr ke aage jeet hai.'*
    c. Lock yourself in a dark room and never come out
2. How experimental are you when it comes to your hair:
    a. Helloooooo! You were the first to sport pink hair colour amongst your friends
    b. Religiously change your look once a year
    c. You've had the same hairstyle since kindergarten
3. Your boyfriend kisses you on the cheek in public. You:
    a. Throw your arms around him and coo, 'I love you too, laav!'
    b. Are kind of embarrassed but give his hand a little squeeze nevertheless
    c. Cringe and think, 'I don't like this barbaric behaviour.'

4. Someone screams at you for no apparent fault of yours. You:
   a. Scream right back and break a plate on their head
   b. Wait for them to calm down and then put your point across
   c. Study your toes and think, 'I had it coming.'
5. When you speak, people usually:
   a. Wear earmuffs
   b. Compliment you on your sing-song tone
   c. Wonder if they've gone deaf

If you've scored mostly As: Heyyyy Hothead, go easy on that aggression. You are a Type A personality. Strong, bold, confident. While it's great being all those things, sometimes it helps to be humble, to extend a listening ear—you know, occasionally. Honestly, being all hyper all the time is so not good for health.

If you've scored mostly Bs: You are one level-headed creature. Congratulations! You speak up when you need to, and stay mum when you have to. Good going, love. Just make sure you continue to stay that way.

If you've scored mostly Cs: You are a doormat. Seriously kiddo, you need to pull your socks up. Take a good hard look at your life and ask yourself: is that what god put you on earth for? To be trampled upon? No, right? So get up, speak up, stop apologizing and show the world you are made of sterner stuff.

Rinki Tripathi scored mostly Bs.

Chapter 1

BlackBerry Messenger Status: Why can't all Mausijis be like the one in *Sholay*???

Rinki Tripathi's got a cell? Lucky gal! Before such thoughts cross your mind, let me clear the air. I was not one of those lucky teens who were gifted cells (fancy or otherwise) by their parents. Boo hoo ☹. So I did what I could. Borrowed my (techno-unsavvy) mom's cell from time to time.

There, that's one thing off my chest. Now for the BBM status.

Well, don't you just love old people? And I don't-mean people over thirty. I mean, really, really old people. I totally did. I mean, I was 100% sure Mausiji was going to be this cute, cuddly, roly-poly grandma type. She'd dunk generous amounts of stinky oil in my hair, make smelly ghee paranthas for me—you know the drill.

Boy, was I in for a rude shock! For starters, Mausiji didn't *look* that old. Her hair was jet black, for crying out loud. (Black Rose Kaali Mehendi, as I found out later). Where was the gummy smile? Where was the shock of white hair? Why, she wasn't even wearing a white blouse-less sari, for god's sake!

'This is little Rinki,' Dad said, by way of introduction.

Here it comes, I thought. The customary cheek pulling accompanied by the time-honoured dialogue, 'My, my, how tall you've grown. You were knee-high when I last saw you.' I mean, it must be there in the Distant Relative Manual.

Well, I couldn't have been more wrong. She gave me a once-over and said, 'I can see where she gets her build from . . .' She tossed a meaningful look in Mom's direction.

Okay, so, Mom's family is a bit on the heavier side. Cough, cough. That's putting it politely. As for, Dad's side, everyone pretty much looks like those stick figures. (Interesting aside: During his childhood, Dad was kept on a staple diet of junk food: samosas, pakoras, chaat, just so he'd beef up. Didn't help. Sigh, some people are just so lucky!)

Mom smiled brightly and said, 'Mausiji, you must be starving. Why don't you freshen up? I'll set the table in a jiffy.'

I really expected Mausiji to shuffle all the way to the room. BUT she marched with all the briskness of an army major. I bet if we practised taekwondo together, she'd be the one throwing me over her shoulder.

Perhaps she was hungry. Yes, that'd explain the brisk walk. My people are known to get real cranky if meals aren't served at regular intervals.

Speaking of meals, that's what Mom had ordered. Mini meals. Fresh from Saravana Bhawan: curd rice, sambhar rice, tomato rice, beans *poriyal*, chips and kesari.

Mausiji looked at the spread much like a medical intern examining a cadaver.

'We love south Indian food,' beamed Mom. By 'we' she meant herself, of course. I was off rice. For life. And while I had long gotten over my dislike for all things sambhary, I wouldn't exactly turn cartwheels at the prospect of having it for breakfast, lunch and dinner.

Mausiji looked as if Mom had jammed a huge idli down her throat. She got to her feet. 'I think I've some aloo paranthas left from the journey.'

'Aloo paranthas? Wow! I'll have them too,' Dad exulted, the corners of his mouth lifting all the way uppp.

Mom's face fell by the exact same proportions. And by the time we were through with lunch, it was also the colour of thunder.

Mausiji retired to her room. That's when Mom let Dad have it.

'I can't believe these women.'

'What women?' Dad asked, looking left and then right.

'The women of your family.'

'Why, what did Rinki do now?'

Mom went on as if she hadn't heard him. 'All they do is find fault. Your mausiji, I tell you . . .'

'Mausiji didn't find fault with you.'

'She criticized my choice of lunch. Lunch I ordered with my own two hands!' Mom said theatrically. 'Doesn't she have anything better to do?'

Apparently not. Meenakshi Mausiji's son and DIL (daughter-in-law, not heart) lived in the US. She spent six months a year with them. For the rest of the time, she was like the wind. She could go anywhere she liked and do anything she pleased.

'Stop overreacting, Sheena,' Dad said dismissively.

Uhhhh-ogaaayyy. That was about as much family drama I could stomach. I jumped to my feet.

'Mom, Dad, I am off. Catching up with Sriram and Robin.'

Sriram lived on the fifth floor of our building. He was the straightest arrow ever. It is one crazy story how we became friends. He had the hots for me, I had the hots for TJ, TJ had the hots for . . . Let's not go there, okay?

As for Robin, she was my bestest friend in Chennai. I say Chennai, because my BFF, is, was, and always will be Ankita. But she lived far, far away in Delhi—making Robin my go-to gal in Chennai. Sometimes I felt as if I was cheating on Ankita, if you know what I mean.

So, Sriram Anna and Robin were seeing each other. Yeah, they were an official I-love-you-you-love-me couple. Would you believe it? The three of us had a little, um, misunderstanding last year. But all's well that ends well, right? At the moment, we were thick as thieves. I mean, we kind of did everything together. By everything, I don't mean EVERYTHING. Don't be gross!

Quick clarification: My relationship with Sriram has always been strictly platonic. Come to think of it, my relationship with most boyfriends has been strictly platonic. Well, almost. Perhaps 2011 would change that. Sigh.

Coming back to my friends, something happened to Robin. Something good. And she went from Plain Jane to Periya Pista (Okay, that's the Tamil slang for 'big shot'). From Miss Curd Rice to Cutie Pie. From Chammathu Payan (Tamil slang for 'good girl') to Cool Cat. Courtesy, her new stylist. Me. Applause please! As my latest darlin' Farhan Akhtar would say, 'Thankoooz the very much.'

True story this. Robin used to be the kind of brainy babe who believed in shaving her head off, growing her underarm hair, that kind of thing. She never, ever cared what others thought of her. But that was *before* she fell for Sriram.

Don't get me wrong. Sriram was no Rambo in the macho department. Or Ranbir in the looks department. But did he care? Nope, nahi, *ille*. He was happy being Mr Super Skinny, all spindly legs and oily hair, parallely playing Romeo.

That's the thing about girls. They can be super smart and all that, but unless they're admired for their looks, they feel as if something's missing.

Like Robin told me, 'My life's all about the 3 Bs—Books, braids, baggy clothes.'

Like I told her, 'Don't let the three Bs kill you. Allow me to help.'

She did. And voila! I designed this special Makeover Programme for her. Trust me, I felt like Sonam in *Aisha* as I played fairy godmother to her. As makeovers go, it was prettyyyy easy.

First Stop:
Chennai's swankiest salon, Toni 'n' Guy at Express Avenue Mall. Haircut by the senior most stylist. I bet he had to use garden shears to cut her frizzy, unkempt mane. But in the end, it was worth it. Really. A snip here, a snip there, and Robin didn't look like Robin any more. She looked more like Rihanna. Okay, Rihanna's distant cousin. But someone more *real*, for sure.

While we were at it, I'd gone as far as to suggest a change of name. You know, a cool name to go with her mane. But she put her foot down. Oh, well, we can't have everything.

On the bright side, she agreed to thread her moustache AND her beard. For the first time ever. Thank you, god. That and a good massage later, she looked totally human.

(Rinki fun fact: Personally, I find massages a little icky. All that oil and cream and goo. Plus, unless you've waxed, you don't really want to show 'em your legs. Usually, it's these PYTs (pretty young things) who do it. They look so damn groomed that you can't really walk in there looking like a scruffy gorilla.

Which brings us to Life's Greatest Mystery #1: How do people go to a parlour looking as if they don't need to go to a parlour?)

Second Stop:
Cosmetics section of Lifestyle, where Robin got a free demo by a funkily dressed make-up artist. She taught Robin how to apply liner and kohl so that her eyes would look bigger. She also showed her how to contour her jaw so that her chin would look smaller. And that made me wonder: Why didn't the big make-up artist in the sky get it right in the first place???

Third Stop
Love Girl boutique. Got Robin a couple of jeggings, knee-length tunics, kaftan tops, a couple of belts, and heels in black, brown and nude shades.

Fourth Stop
Destination: Levi's Store.
   Mission: Shopping for jeans.
   Goof-up: Inviting Sriram for this all-important mission.

'Size 30 should be okay for you, no?' I asked Robin, taking in her, err, girth.

Her face turned a bright shade of red.

'I think size 28 should do,' inserted Sriram loyally.

'Sriram, puhleeeze. Let the pro handle it,' I interjected, giving Robin a little shove in the direction of the changing room. Five minutes later, there was no sign of her. We put our ear to the door.

Grunt. Groan. Huff. Puff. Pant. Pant.

Sriram and I exchanged worried glances.

'She sounds as if she is in pain,' Sriram said in alarm.

I patted his arm.

Thumppppp!

At that point, I had no choice but to barge into the changing room.

Okay, so I was a little off the mark. Robin's waist size was 32.

'Same as mine,' chirped Sriram.

Moral of the story? Robin needed to go on a diet. Like yesterday.

I know, I know, I wasn't exactly size zero myself. Thighs the size of Thailand. Hips that could put yesteryear Bollywood actresses to shame. But what the hell! I didn't have a boyfriend. Nor was I in the movies. I didn't have to be a certain size or look a certain way. I was a free agent. If I wanted to stuff my face and pile on the pounds, I certainly could.

Sigh. It was all up to me. I had to do it. I had to make the final sacrifice. I simply had to drag Robin to the gym. My motives were strictly altruistic. And no, it had nothing to do with Mausiji's snide comments on my weight ('My my, looks like Chennai's suiting you, Rinki').

Simply put, the canvas had to be ready for the artist's work to be admired. Unless Robin got the body, how would she do justice to my work? Let's hear it for Rinki, guys! The world's greatest stylist.

So it was decided. We'd go to the gym together. The guru and the shishya, the master and the disciple, Master Shifu and Po.

Final Destination, er, in a manner of speaking:
'How about Pink Fitness Gym? An exclusive gym for women . . .' Robin suggested, checking out their website.

I cancelled the plan outright. I mean, think about it.

Working out: Boring!

Working out without boys: Bloody boooooringgggg!

So, Fitness One gym it was.

P.S. Turns out, people are right. Gyms are useless. Robin, Sudha and I hit the gym religiously. For two weeks. And didn't lose ONE single gram. But it wasn't a total waste because that's where I met Google.

Rinki Tripathi is taking an online quiz on Teenz Forever.

Quiz Number #411. Is it friendship or love?
1. A certain someone of the opposite sex (ACSOTOS) asks you if you're free on Saturday. You:
   a. Say you're going clubbing and ask him to join you
   b. Cautiously ask him what he has in mind

c.　Sneeze and pretend you're coming down with something

2.　ACSOTOS compliments you on the clothes you are wearing. You:

a.　Have visions of a beach wedding

b.　Blush and say 'Really, this old top?'

c.　Say 'You could use some style tips yourself.'

3.　ACSOTOS whistles as a pretty girl walks past. You:

a.　Think he has bad taste

b.　Stay mum

c.　Whistle louder than him

4.　ACSOTOS offers to pay for a shared meal. You:

a.　Look very pleased and push your wallet back into your purse

b.　Protest half-heartedly

c.　Snatch the bill from his hands and insist on going Dutch

5.　ACSOTOS calls you late in the night. You're dead tired but you:

a.　Answer at the first ring

b.　Talk but yawn all through

c.　Put the phone on silent mode and go back to sleep

If you've scored mostly As. Girl, you are so in 'lau'! Congrats. It's why you wake up smiling, go to bed grinning and generally have a stupid expression on your face all day. What you need to do is act on those feelings. Just crushing won't do, girl. It's time you made a move.

If you've scored mostly Bs: You're in the friend zone. But it could move either way. You could fall for the dude or settle down into a tame friendship, who knows? So see a lot of each other, spend quality time together, get to know each other well. And oh, have fun. Clear hai?

If you've scored mostly Cs: You are so detached, so not into him, it's cruel. We're not sure if you even like the guy. Just kidding. Go on, enjoy your friendship. Without a fear in the world that it will lead to anything more. But we're guessing you already know that.

Rinki Tripathi scored mostly Bs.

Chapter 2

BBM Status Message: Just met my doppelgänger! Give or take a few 'vital' body parts ☺

The wolf pack (after *The Hangover*, that's how I thought of Robin, Sudha and meself) had enrolled into Fitness One, the super swanky neighbourhood gym.

On our first day, I found Google. Or rather, Google found me.

I was spinning away to glory on my exercise bike, when I heard a lamb bleating. I looked over my shoulder, but saw nothing.

'Baaa . . .'

I cocked an ear in the direction of the sound.

'Baaachao! Helpp!'

No, I certainly wasn't hearing things.

'Overrr here,' came a voice that could dub for Sachin in all those TV commercials.

I swung my leg off the bike.

There it was, partially hidden from view, the fattened lamb getting slaughtered. Lying on a bench, grappling with what looked like 100-kg weights. First look at Google. His arms were shaking uncontrollably. His cheeks were enormous balloons about to burst. His damp hair was plastered to his forehead.

I ran to the trainer, who was busy flirting with Miss I-Live-On-Celery-Sticks-and-I-Have-the-Ass-To-Show-For-It. (Life's Greatest Mystery #2: Why do skinny chicks enrol into a gym if they are so not interested in doing an honest day's workout?)

'Excuse me,' I began.

He swatted me away like a pesky fly.

'Hey!' I cried out, playing two dumb-bells like dandiya sticks in mid-air.

That got his attention. 'Hey, Armstrong, you need to work on those,' he drawled, gesturing at my wobbly arms.

Really, now. I always thought my arms were my best feature. (Trust me, from there, it's aaaall downhill!) Listening to the trainer, the ugly truth hit me. There *were* no best features. Sob!

With my heart as heavy as my thighs, I led him to Grappling Google. He bent down and *cliccccckkkk*! In one swift motion, he yanked the weights off.

An out-of-breath Google pulled himself to sitting position. I thrust my water bottle at him.

'Hey, are you okay?'

He nodded, panting.

'Hi, I'm Rinki. And you are?'

'Don't you know who I am?'

'World-famous in Chennai, are you?' I said archly.

That drew a chuckle out of him. He raised his hands in mock surrender.

'Let's start over. I'm Google.'

'Google?'

'If I don't know something, chances are, neither does the search engine,' he said modestly. 'Only my parents call me Jugal Varma.'

'I'm Tripathi. Rinki Tripathi. Tell me, Google, what brings a good guy like you to a gym like this?'

'My bad luck . . . pant pant . . . My folks, my sis, my friends, the whole universe . . . pant pant . . . Everyone had a problem with my weight . . . my daily calorie intake . . . dammit . . . I just wanted to get them off my back, machan.'

At that point, it struck me. This guy could be my brother!

Right on cue, Robin and Sudha appeared on the scene. I introduced them to Google.

After he ambled away, I turned to Robin. 'Are you thinking what I am thinking?'

'Yeah,' she replied, her head bobbing. 'Bugger needs to work out. Big time.'

'Not that, Robin. Doesn't he remind you of someone?'

She thought for a moment. 'That smart alec in the Sprite ads?'

'Oh, forget it.'

Now, had I wished for a brother, god had listened to me, all right. I mean, we could have separated in some mela seventeen years ago. I mentally tabulated our similarities.

Rinki	Google
Weight-challenged	Weight-challenged
Weird hair	Weird hair
Opinionated	Opinionated
Hates working out	Hates working out
Whiny	Whiny

Did either of my parents have an affair and parcel him off to their friends?

To make things worse, Mom was watching *Masoom* when I reached home. You know, the movie where the hero has an affair and brings home his illegit son. He tries to pass him off as his (you guessed it) 'friend's son'. Yuck!

Mom was glued to the screen, a packet of potato chips in her hand.

As far as Mom's concerned, transfats and triglycerides are something out of *Harry Potter* and *The Lord of the Rings* novels. Pure fantasy!

As Naseer and the li'l boy sang soppy songs in a scenic hill station, I felt compelled to kick-start the conversation.

'What a jerk,' I said, reaching into the bag of chips.

'Yeah.'

That was encouraging.

'I asked him for Bingo Mad Angles and he gave me this boring packet of chips,' Mom continued.

'Whaaatttt?'

'That Pandian Store chap,' Mom replied nonchalantly. Pandian Store. It's where we got all our monthly supplies from.

'Noooo, Mom, I mean, this character on screen. Isn't he a complete loser? Imagine lying to his wifey about his illegit son.'

'Mmmm.' Mom was clearly concentrating more on the snack than on the screen.

I plucked the distraction out of her hand.

'Heyyyy,' Mom yelped, desperately trying to clutch at the bag of chips but coming up with a handful of air.

'Mom! Please, let's give it a break.'

'Okay, we will watch the rest of the movie tomorrow.'

I sighed. 'I meant the chips, Mom.'

'Shhh, I am concentrating on the dialogue.'

We watched for the next fifteen minutes in complete silence.

When I couldn't take it any longer, I tried another tack.

'What's wrong with the heroine? Why is she taking her anger out on the poor kid?'

Mom clucked in sympathy.

'I mean, it's not his fault his parents had an affair.'

Mom nodded.

'These things happen.'

'Absolutely,' Mom chimed in. 'Krishna is seeing Dhanya, you know. And he is married to Rashi.'

Outrageous! There was an extramarital affair happening in Mom's friend circle and she hadn't bothered to tell me.

'Which aunty is Dhanya again?' I asked Mom, my eyes ablaze with the anticipation of gossip.

'The one in *Mera Sasural Sirf Mera Hai*.'

Oh. Rrrright. A stupid serial on prime-time TV. Mom had just started watching it, courtesy, who else, Mausiji! All day long, the two ladies watched mopey soaps. At other times, they watched reruns of mopey soaps.

No wonder Mom had become like this. If I had to watch people getting slapped three times in slow motion, I'd go bananas too.

'Anyway, Rinki, I'm sleepy. Have a busy day tomorrow.'

'Kirtan kitty?' I asked.

Mom nodded.

Did I tell you about Mom's kirtan kitty? It's where all these women met to sing hymns in praise of god for the first five minutes. Of course, they sang 'praises' of lesser mortals for the next fifty.

Back to moi. It's only when I met Google's family that I finally decided he couldn't be IT. My half-bro, that is.

Google's mother was also the mother of all socialites. I mean, she was a member of every club in Chennai. She was hardly ever home. Always out as she was for a:

1. Kitty party
2. Round table meet
3. Ladies' Club AGM
4. Rotary Club meeting
5. Wine and cheese evening
6. Book/store/designer line launch
7. Any other social event you can think of

And his dad, gawd. He was sooooo loud. In terms of his voice *and* his clothes. Shudder! Bet they had to replace all the mirrors and bulbs in the house every other day.

Google was also a proud brother. More on his sister later.

We were peas in two completely different pods. That's it.

BTW, that was the second bro scare in my life. Back when I was in the IX grade, a friend of mine was given a nasty surprise by her folks. In the form of a sibling. Can you imagine! I spent months worrying about it. I mean, I could have never, ever lived down the embarrassment. Thank god, Mom and Dad spared me the blushes.

Rinki Tripathi is taking an online quiz on Teenz Forever.

Online Quiz # 456. Are your parents ruining your life?

1. When you count your best friends, do you include your parents?
   a. Yes, why wouldn't I?
   b. Eeeks! I'm not crazy, dude
   c. Don't know/can't say

2. Do you turn to your parents for style advice?
   a. Sure do. They've great taste
   b. What do you think I am? Nuts?
   c. Don't know/can't say

3. Do your parents decide who your friends are?
   a. Absolutely. They are so knowledgeable and worldly-wise
   b. No way in hell
   c. Don't know/can't say

4. Does parental approval mean a lot to you?
   a. Duh, it is the most important thing in the world
   b. Parental approval? What's that?
   c. Don't know/can't say

5. What do you want to be when you grow up?
   a. Ask Mom and Dad
   b. Do I have to? Grow up, I mean
   c. Don't know/can't say

If you've scored mostly As: You worship the ground your parents walk on. In fact, they walk all over you. Dude, better get some personality. You are not your parents. Yes, your parents are great, they love you and they know the ways of the world, but still. You gotta live your own life. Cut the cord, will ya?

If you've scored mostly Bs: You are a typical teen. Hang in there. Parents can be difficult but they mean well. Well, mostly. It is a good thing you don't let them ride roughshod over your feelings, but remember they have your best interests at heart. No point being a rebel without a cause (or one without a pause).

If you've scored mostly Cs: What the hell is wrong with you? Make up your mind at least about one thing in life. Yes, life is tough. Yes, you have to make choices. No, no one else will make them for you. Jeez! What's with all that indecision?

Rinki Tripathi scored mostly Bs.

Chapter 3

BlackBerry Status Message: Oh, the evils of social media networking!

'Rinki?'

It was my name all right but it took me by surprise. It was, after all, Meanie Mausi, oops, Meenakshi Mausi addressing me.

Mausiji addressing *me*! Most days she pretended I didn't exist. Hard to do in a three-bedroom flat. Harder to do when it concerns a fully grown teen. So you can imagine how stunned I was when she actually called out my name.

'Yeah?' I said, a bit unsure.

'Teach me how to use the computer,' she said, attempting to pass off her bared fangs as a smile.

Was that her way of asking for a favour, I wondered. With Mausiji, one could never tell. She always sounded like she was barking an order to particularly dim-witted folk. As in, Mom and moi.

'The computer?' I asked, a bit startled.

'You know, that thing you work on . . .'

'Rinki knows what a computer is, Mausiji,' Mom cut in, gliding into the room. 'In fact, she regularly reads faces on the computer.'

'Really?' Mausiji looked all ears.

No, not really. She meant Facebook. Sorry, Mark Zuckerberg. But you know how daft parents can be.

'Er, Mom, it's not really reading faces. It's more of a social networking site . . .'

And for the next half an hour I proceeded to show them the wonders of the Internet.

The three of us had such a good time (showing off and learning, respectively) that we repeated the session over the next one week.

At the end of it, I almost changed my vocation. From fashion stylist to primary school teacher. From dispenser of style tips to promoter of wisdom. From Style Goddess to Gyaan Guru.

I actually thought the computer sessions had gone quite well until I received the following notifications:

Sheena Tripathi wants to be friends on FB.
Meenakshi Chaturvedi wants to be friends on FB.

Like I said, something good came out of the whole gym experience. I had company: a person who hated working out as much as I did. Google. One whine session led to another. And soon we were pretttttyy good friends. Here's what drew us closer.

Google's sister Neha was participating in Miss Teen Chennai. The Beauty Pageant with a Difference. Oh, it was just their baseline. There was nothing 'different' about it. Like all beauty pageants, it was about three things: Looks, looks and looks.

Good for her. Neha was tall, slim and cute in a pale sort of a way. Kind of like Bella in *Twilight*. A walking-talking Fair and Lovely ad. (If her parents ever put her up for adoption, my relatives back in Delhi would sure as hell adopt her. It's unfair how much those guys luuuuurve all things fair.)

Anyhoo, I'd confessed my love for styling to Google during one of our gym sessions. So, when Neha decided to enter the pageant, Google put her on to me. Zimble.

I was at their place, a spanking new apartment complex at Kilpauk.

'Here's the brief, Rinki. I want my clothes to be stylish, flattering, hep. But, (a) Nothing too deep at the back; (b) Nothing too short at the hem; (c) Nothing too low in the front.'

'So, essentially, you want to wear a biiiiiig jute bag,' I retorted.

'Come on, ya. Don't tell me only revealing stuff can look good,' Neha said with a shake of the head.

And who made her the expert again?

'Neha, Neha, Neha, do *not* let your sacrifices go down the drain.'

'What sacrifices?'

'Google tells me that you've been on all sorts of diets. Don't you remember how it felt? Going without food for days on end? Skipping solids? Chomping on celery sticks? Giving those yummy pakoras a miss?'

'Oh, it was terrible! That's why I was eating them on the sly all through.'

I continued as if I hadn't heard her. 'Don't you remember the hardships? Standing quietly in the shadows, watching everyone pig out at dessert counters?'

Neha jabbed a finger to her chest. 'Pigging out at dessert counters, that was me.'

'You've worked so hard, Neha. Well, it's payback time now,' I said, my eyes shining.

'If I show my body, there'll be hell to pay,' she retorted, flicking open her wallet and pointing to a grim-looking young man. Her boyfriend Ajay.

'Will you let a *guy* come in between you and your dreams, Neha?'

'Guys,' Google piped up, stepping in between Neha and moi, 'you're missing the point. This is a great opportunity. We shouldn't blow it.'

'We won't blow it. Trust me, ya,' Neha said confidently.

I sighed. I was fighting a losing battle with Hansel and Gretel here. Neha was acting like a Bollywood starlet who wanted to climb to the top *and* keep her clothes on. I mean, it's common knowledge. Clothes and success are inversely proportional to each other. Check out Ash in *Dhoom-2*, Priyanka in *Fashion*, Bips in most of her films.

I could go on and on. But the Princess of Prude snapped me back to reality.

'Let's go through the rounds. We'll zero in on the number of costumes,' Neha said. 'Okay, so there are four rounds. 'Prelims, catwalk, talent, question-answer. That's four outfits.

So what do I wear for each? Any suggestions, guys?' Neha looked about the room.

That made me uncomfy. I was the official stylist. Heck, I was the *only* stylist in the room! So the question should have been directed solely at me.

Google was a stranger to fashion. He was like Anne Hathway in *The Devil Wears Prada*. I swear! His idea of ishtyle was to live in slogan T-shirts. Even Sania Mirza had stopped wearing them, for god's sake. The T-shirt he had on at the moment, for instance, proudly proclaimed: 'If you like me, raise your hands. If you don't, raise your standards.' I rest my case.

I, on the other hand, was like Meryl Streep, Anne's boss, the style expert. I just hoped our local Farhan 'n' Zoya realized as much.

'How about a kurti and leggings for the first round?' Neha said after a while.

'Neha, we are talking "beauty pageant" and not "snore fest".'

Neha clammed up.

'Okay, let's see. You've got to make a good first impression. So why don't we go with something that flatters your figure? You have a slender waist, narrow hips . . .'

I turned the pages of the magazine swiftly and stabbed a finger at a pic.

'There, that's perfect: The cream and black creation. Minimal accessories. That's your look.'

Neha looked doubtful. 'Won't the cream make me look washed out? How about a darker shade? Some bling?'

That's the problem with people in our country. When they dress up, they go all out. They wear everything they have in their closet. The brightest colours, tonnes of make-up, all their jewellery. Result? They end up looking like a store window.

'We're not aiming for the Christmas-tree effect here, Neha,' I muttered as patiently as I possibly could. 'We want to go in for an understated, classy look.'

'People don't know all this "understated-wonderstated". In India, it's called the dull look,' Neha pouted.

'Trust me on this one, Neha. Would you please?'

She looked unconvinced but nodded all the same.

'Great,' I exulted.

'I was thinking of veena in the talent round,' Neha said without warning.

'Who's Veena?' I said without thinking.

'Veena, the musical instrument. I want to play it in the talent round,' Neha said wryly.

'The veena, of course,' I said, feigning a little cough.

Some people, I tell you. No sense of humour.

'Okay, so why don't I wear a churidaar in the prelims?'

'Neha, puhleeeeeze! Next you will want to wear a *pattu* saree.'

'Why can't she wear a sari?' Google butted in. 'Vidya Balan does it all the time.'

'Vidya wears Sabyasachi sarees, guys. They cost a bomb. And you have to complete the look. The jhumkis . . .'

'I can borrow Mom's.'

'The potlis . . .'

'Naani has several.'

That's one hep granny you got there, Neha, I thought with grudging admiration.

'The big bindis.'

'We can get them from those small stalls at Pondy Bazaar.'

'Okie! But where will you get the Sabya from?'

'What, ya?'

'Sabya as in Sabyasachi. Oh, never mind. And please, stop saying "ya". It sounds totally DM.'

'DM?'

'Downmarket,' I explained

'Okay, ya,' Neha replied solemnly.

Neha's Final Outfits:

1. Prelims—Baby pink ruffled dress with a beige bolero (from Rinki's closet, altered to her size)
2. Catwalk—Wine coloured floor-length gown (soon to be bought)
3. Talent round—Anarkali suit (model's own)
4. Question-answer round—Same as Round Two (in a different cut and colour)

Now we needed to go buy these. See, the thing about Chennai is that it's not Delhi. And shopping options are very—how do I put it delicately—limited. No limit to how much you can crib about it, though. You have two halfway decent malls, couple of standalone boutiques and that's it. Shopping overrrr.

In Delhi, if I set out to shop, I could shop all day without running out of places. But like Dad said, we were not in Delhi any more. Sigh.

Rinki Recommends

Shopping Destinations in Chennai:

1. Express Avenue Mall (All of Chennai shops and loiters—mostly loiters—here.)

2. Citi Centre Mall (Took a beating because of aforementioned mall but let's give credit where it's due. The air conditioning is wayyyy superior.)
3. Pondy Bazaar (Kind of like Janpanth. Stuff's real cheap, value for money.)
4. Tiny boutiques (Pricey, but who's complaining.)
5. Export surplus shops (These are a real find. You've to dig and dig but I've unearthed many a treasure in there.)

Psst. There are a few smaller malls and stand-alone branded stores, but we are not talking borrrrinnggg here, are we?

BTW, I told Mom I wanted to be a personal shopper when I grow up. And she was soooo cross. She didn't speak to me that whole evening. Said she didn't want me to become 'someone's maid'. Asked me why couldn't I be something more dignified, something like an investment banker? Like her cousin's son.

I mean, heyyylooo! If a personal shopper is a maid then what's an investment banker? I mean, we are both spending someone else's money for them, right? And thanks to the recession, sooner or later, all investment bankers will be out of work. But people will still need to wear clothes. If you ask me, it's personal shoppers who'll go laughing all the way to the bank.

Life's Greatest Mystery #3: Why do parents love complicating life? It's Youngistan's future that hangs in the balance, after all. So why can't they just take a chill pill? Why can't they see the lighter side of life? Why must they do everything on the basis of 'how things look' as opposed to 'how things feel'?

Take Mom, for instance.

1. If she has to wear so-and-so outfit, her first thought is 'who else will wear what'
2. If she has to admit her daughter in some school, her first reaction is 'who else sends their kids here'
3. If she has to go some place for a holiday, a holiday for god's sake, she goes 'who else has gone there'

Jeez! Who the hell cares?

I tell you, when I'm eighteen, I'm going to live as I damn well please.

Back to the pageant.

Neha got knocked out early. But she did manage to win the Best Costume Award. I think she could've easily been in the Top 10. If only she had kept her cool. If only she hadn't muffed up in the Q & A round. But no, she had to go ahead and prove that she was Google's sis! Sigh. Not everyone can look good and speak well and dress great and be confident. Guess I'm an exception. LOL!

Anyway, I wanted to run up on stage and give my long* rehearsed Oscar acceptance speech. I could totally relate to all our movie directors. It's they who do all the hard work and the actor walks away with all the compliments.

Coming back to the KBC (Kaun Banega Catwalk Queen) round, it was a piece of cake. If you know your beauty pageants, that is. See for yourself:

Judge's question: If there were many starving children around, whom would you feed first and why?

Rocket science, anyone?

Neha's answer (hold on your horses): 'I'll do inky-pinky-ponky.'

Yes, Neha actually said that.

I mean, you can't win Miss Pondy Bazaar with that!

Like I told Neha, it was a trick question. And trick questions (like all those questions our parents spring on us) should never be answered. They have to be wisely deflected, neatly sidestepped. She really should've said, 'God lives in children so I'd make sure they were ALL well fed and burping away to eternity. Blah blah.' Or words to that effect.

Anyway, that was THE END of Neha's 'I want to be Mother Teresa when I grow up' phase. But her folks, they were mighty thrilled. Google actually got up on his seat and jiggled his ass. The rest of her family burst into loud cheers. Gawd! It reminded me of that scene in DDLJ. You know, where SRK tells his dad he flunked and his dad's chest swells up with pride.

Some people are so easy to please, I tell you.

*Rinki Tripathi's Oscar Acceptance Speech (until the biggie, also applicable for chintoo award ceremonies)

Oh, wow! An Oscar. *(choking on the words)*. I-I-I don't know what to say.

Sound of static. Justin Timberlake, who's giving the award, gallantly steps in to help. He proffers a pristine white handkerchief. Rinki duly blows her nose into it and hands it back to him.

Thank you, Justin. *(Blows a kiss to him. He catches it and puts it in his tuxedo pocket.)*

Snort. Sniffle.

I'd like to thank god, Mom and Dad . . . Mom, where are you? *(Shielding her eyes)* I can't see you. Even in that fire-engine red suit of yours. Oh, there you are! Okay, stop jumping up and down now; you're embarrassing me. Thanks so much for all the love, hugs and kisses; a few good genes would've been nice, too.

Dad, I know you're still at work. Hope Citibank has given you a smallish TV in the cubicle you call home, so you can see me live and exclusive. This is what I look like now. Been what, five years since we last met?

Ankita, Robin, Sudha, Google: Mwaah mwaaah mwaaah for being the bestest friends anyone can ask for. (Like Farhan said in ZNMD, 'Send the cheque home').

Thank you to my very own life-support mechanism—Sakku Bai, Maheshwari, all my hired help down the ages. It's true, behind every successful woman, there is a woman cooking and cleaning for her.

A biiig thank you to all my teachers. Especially the ones who couldn't wait to see me go far. Here I am. In LA. Now, keep those autograph books ready. Who's complaining about my handwriting now!

Thank you, Madonna, Rihanna, Victoria, Katrina, Kareena, Hrithik and Ranbir for giving me the opportunity to style you. I owe a good deal of my success to you guys. Mwaahhh! Thank you, Robert. Look forward to styling you in *Twilight's* tenth sequel. And no, I won't let you down. Even if you're forty and still single, I'll marry you. Happy?

Rest of you Hollywoodies, will see you at the after-party at Leonardo's beach house. Cheerio!

Rinki Tripathi is taking an online quiz on Teenz Forever.

Online Quiz # 511. How ambitious are you?

1. After the finals, your classmates ask you, 'What next? You say:
   a. Coffee
   b. Undergrad course in the US
2. When your parents ask you about your future plans, you say:
   a. Exams just got over, for god's sake
   b. Lawyer/surgeon/engineer/techie
3. If your teachers could describe you in a few words, they'd choose:
   a. Gone case
   b. Will go far
4. How important is it for you to do better than your peers:
   a. Pears, the soap?
   b. It's my mission in life
5. What is your life's goal?
   a. Goals? Are we talking soccer here?
   b. To be rich, successful and famous

If you've scored mostly As: Good grief! Your lack of ambition is frightening. You need to go to a career counsellor ASAP. Surely you are good at something? Anything? Being laid-back is one thing, but this is bordering on the ridiculous. Get a grip. And soon.

If you've scored mostly Bs: Well, good for you. You know where you are headed and which road will take you there. You have mapped out the rest of your life in your head, oh yeah! Just a note of caution, don't get carried away by the career currents. There's more to life than being successful. Let us know when you find out what it is.

Rinki Tripathi scored mostly As.

To-do List for XII Grade (according to Rinki)

1. Buy a cell (heyloo, I needed a mobile phone like yesterday)
2. Collect enough dough to buy a BlackBerry (An iPhone will do just fine as well. God, are you listening?)
3. Join a gym
4. Lose weight (Plan A, the gym was soooo not working out. Enter Plan B)
5. Plan another trip to Delhi (Need those gorgeous palazzo pants from Zara)
6. Collect enough dough to buy palazzo pants from Zara
7. Get hair straightened (Only thing to have made it to my to-do list two years in a row. How sad is that?)
8. Get a cool tattoo
9. Get a temporary job or something (How on earth am I going to afford all the above?)
10. Get a hot BF (or what in the world will I do with the cell, the weight loss, the killer clothes, the lustrous hair et al.?)

To-do List for XII Grade (according to Mom and Dad)

1. Study for Board Exams
2. Study for Board Exams
3. Study for Board Exams

Chapter 4

BlackBerry Messenger Status: The birds, the bees, and poor ole Me.

Quick fact: Indian parents are pushy.

Exactly how pushy, I got to experience first-hand one sultry afternoon. School had just about opened.

There I was, perfectly happy with my existence when they accosted me. It happened to be a long weekend. (Translation: Dad was in town.) And naturally, Mom thought it'd be a good idea to 'have the talk'.

I was summoned to the living room.

I plopped on to the couch, a glass of nimboo paani in my hand.

Dad sat down heavily on the centre table, a grave expression on his face. Mom looked as if she was going to join him. Mercifully enough, she thought the better of it.

My eyes swung to the TV screen. A Hrithik number had just come on. Gawd, he was hot. The way his jeans fit him around the hips. So snug . . .

'I know what you're thinking.'

'You do?' I sputtered, nearly choking on my drink.

'It's time we had the talk,' Mom added.

And suddenly, I was super tense.

The Talk? They were going to do it?! My parents were going to take the plunge?! Talk to me about the birds and the bees?! Oh gosh, I never, ever imagined my parents would discuss sex! I mean, with me.

'You know how it is. You've reached a certain age.'

For god's sake, I wanted to shriek. I'd reached that age years back.

'You should be ready,' Dad continued.

But I don't even have a boyfriend, I screamed silently.

'You should do it.'

'What?!?' I said, nearly popping off the couch like some jack-in-the-box. Surely they didn't mean it. I mean, it just wouldn't be right. Even I wasn't that broad-minded, for god's sake.

'There are so many people your age doing it,' Mom said softly. 'There's nothing wrong in it.'

'You should join their ranks.'

I was aghast.

'I should?'

Mom nodded encouragingly. 'Not as if you haven't done it before.'

Oh, god! This was hysterical. I was hysterical. It couldn't be possible. They had completely lost it. They were actually asking me to do the deed. Then another crippling thought struck me. Were the two of them on dope? I mean, they were sitting so calmly and asking their young bud of a daughter to lose her . . .

'Just go to a reputed person,' Dad continued, sounding alarmingly like that whacko dad in *American Pie* . . .

'Now, that's something your dad and I agree upon.'

That was it. The last straw. I couldn't bear listening to another word.

'Mom, Dad, please! Stopppppppppp!'

'I know what you're thinking. But there's no shame in it.'

'Excuse me!' I exploded. 'I don't know what's gotten into you both but I refuse. I, Rinki Tripathi, simply refuse to go against my morals and principles and . . .'

'What's so immoral about taking tuitions?' Mom wanted to know.

That stopped me dead in my tracks . . . Funny, did someone say tuitions?

'Tuitions?' I repeated slowly. 'As in coaching classes?'

'Yes, tuitions. Why, what did you think?' Dad trailed off, a puzzled look on his face.

'Tuitions! Of course! Heh, heh, heh,' I tittered nervously. Not the first time I'd be taking tuitions, that's for sure.

Mom, however, was not that easily fooled. She had a suspicious expression on her face. I could see her mind working furiously. In reverse, to boot. Desperately trying to play the conversation and fit it to another, far more sinister context.

'I know what you must be thinking,' Dad said, calm as ever.

Believe me, Dad, you haven't a clue. I wanted to kick myself for thinking my parents could be that forward. I mean, that would be the height of broad-mindedness. Kind of like Woodstock in Tripathiland.

'It's only July. Board Exams are way off,' Dad said, breaking into my reverie.

'But I don't need tuitions,' I protested.

'Just like you don't need to come first in class. Just like you don't need a good degree,' Dad retorted.

'But Dad!'

'No ifs and buts. You are going for accounts tuitions. You can go during the weekends, brush up on the basics, get your doubts cleared . . .'

I was fuming by the time Dad finished deciding the rest of my life. Amrish Puri from DDLJ, anyone?

Life's Greatest Mystery #4: Why do parents act so bloody high-handed?

As if we don't know what we want out of life. As if we don't know what is good for us. As if we don't know anything. Bah!

I so didn't want a first class or a B. Com or a BBA degree. I wanted to go to Mumbai. I wanted to work for a fashion magazine (*Cosmo, Vogue, Vanity Fair, Harper's Bazaar* and what have you). Of course, I was dying to style celebs. The bigger the better.

But I didn't say it aloud. Because I turned to look at Mom and she had a funny expression on her face. She hadn't said a word since the misunderstanding had been cleared. I bet she had added two and two and come up with two thousand two hundred and twenty-two. The effect of Mausiji's company, no doubt.

Google Search: Coaching classes for XII grade in Chennai

They say, when it rains, it pours. No kidding. The day after Mom and Dad cracked the tuition whip, so did my English teacher, Anandi Ma'am. She asked me to 'improve my handwriting'. Suggested I write a page every day. Said practice makes one perfect. The Board Exams were around the corner (now, where did I hear that one before?) and I needed to buck up (ditto).

Okay now, to say that my handwriting is bad would be an understatement. But ever since first grade, my teachers had been putting up with it. So I'd kind of forgotten that the problem existed.

Whatte rude reminder of my childhood problem. I so wanted to wiggle out of it. But there was nothing to be done. I broke my head over it all day. What could I possibly write?

List of things I could possibly write every day:

1. Stuff from my textbooks. Yikesssss! How lame would that be?
2. A book. Heck, I'd no patience to do that kind of thing. I wonder how writers do it. Sit holed up in a room, hunched over the comp for days on end. Shudder, shudder. I certainly had better things to do in life.
3. A fashion blog. Yes, that was purrfect! It'd be cool. It'd be simple. It'd hardly take time. I could fill up a page a day talking about fashion. I could even publish it. Yes, that would make me famous! I would have lots of followers around the world. And one day, Shakira would ask me to dress her up for the opening ceremony of the Olympics or something.

And that's how I started writing my blog. The new one. (I'd started one last year but that went kaput. In fact, I'd gotten as far as one highly controversial post and then kind of lost interest. Ho-hum). This one, it'd be different, of course. Second time lucky and all that.

Which brought me to the topic at hand: the name. Okay, so writing the blog seemed to be easier than naming it. But hey, I had to name it right. I couldn't, just couldn't opt for a cheesy name, you know. No way. It had to be something cute, something fun, something fresh, something ME.

Blog Branding Options:

1. Rinki's Rantings? Nah! Had a horrible ring to it.
2. Ringa ringa? (After the hit Telugu song. Same one Salman's 'Dhinka chika' was based on.) Nope. It had to have all-India appeal. Scratch that; international appeal was a must.
3. The Three Rs? (Readable, Real, Rinki?) I dunno. I was kind of iffy about it.

So Batman decided to bounce the thoughts off her trusted lieutenant, Robin.

'Haaaalp me, Robin! I'm so stuck, I tell you. Can't think of a single good name for my blog.'

'Hmmmm,' Robin murmured.

'Robin, puhleeeaaase, I beseech ya.'

'You are one super chick, da,' she replied absent-mindedly. 'I'm sure you'll figure it out.'

'That's it!' I whooped, enveloping Robin into a bear hug.

'W-w-whoa!' Robin gasped, startled.

'Super Chick! Wait a minute, how about Chennai Super Chick? Yup, that's even better! Oh, Robin, you're a lifesaver!'

I planted a huge kiss on her cheeks before hurrying away. 'Whatever, duuuude,' Robin muttered, rolling her eyes. And just like that my blog had a name.

Now came the 'About Me' section. I racked my brains and came up with multiple drafts:

Draft 1:
Hi, I'm Rinki. The newest fashion stylist in town.
Ugghhh.

Draft 2:
Hello! I'm Rinki. Nice to meet you.
Eewww.

Draft 3:
I'm . . .
Arrrghhhhhhhhhhh!

Forget it. I was never going to get started this way. Being a perfectionist can be such a curse, I tell you.

So I decided to stop being picky and write the first thing that came to mind.

Full and Final Draft:
Hi there,

It's me, Chennai Super Chick.

I'm fun, fab and trendy. And I'm here to share some cool life mantras with you. From life to love, from parents to teachers, from fun to fashion, let's discuss everything under the sun.

Let's begin with fashion. While some of you like getting your dose of fashion from books, others get it from TV shows, some others turn to their parents. Shudder, shudder! Well, now you have moi. Your friendly neighbourhood stylist. Your guide to high fashion. I'll be sure to share cool tips with you, rescue you from fashion disasters, and help you channel your inner diva.

Firstly, I believe all of us are born with a sense of style. I mean, just think about those cute rompers you wore as a baby. So, my theory is that we just happen to lose it along the way. Worry not! I am here to bring it back into your lives. With a biiiig bang. And nope, it won't cost you a pie. All I need is your attention. So read every word carefully. Okay?

With time and practice, you'll develop a sense of style of your own, and wow everyone around you. Hell, yeah. So fasten your seatbelts, grab some munchies, and get reading. The fashion fever has just started!!!

Love, hugs, and kisses,

Chennai Super Chick

Post #1

Hello, gurls!

Summer's here. And so is everything summery. So, unless you're living on the other side of the Tropics, it's time to put away your winter gear (quick, get those mothballs). Say bye-bye to those trench coats, mufflers and furry boots, and get set for an all-new wardrobe.

So what are the hottest (pun unintended) trends this season? Check my list out. Snag these styles and be on your way to be crowned Miss Summer Queen. Go, girl!

Let's kick off with the clothes, okay?

What's Hot	**What's Not**
Sundresses in pastel shades	*Knitwear (duh!)*
Oversized shades (Think Hollywood glam)	*Ho-hum sunglasses*
Strappy sandals (The more colourful the better)	*Chunky wedges*
Hats	*Caps (so kindergarten)*
Linen capris	*Corduroys*
Thin, braided belts	*Broad belts*
Short shorts	
Fit-flops, flip-flops, ballerina flats	*Boots*
Cool sling bags	
Hoops	*Danglers*
Colourful beads	

And now for the make-up. Here goes:

Grab it	**Toss it**
Brown kohl pencil	*Black kohl (too harsh for summer)*
Eyeshadow	*Mascara (think raccoon eyes, all that sweat)*
Light sunscreen	*Heavy sunblock*
Pink lip gloss	*Matte lipsticks (ugh!)*
Coral blush-on	*Maroon blush-on (same as above)*
Moisturizer	*Foundation*
Fruity, floral body spray	*Heavy-duty perfume*

Okay, this should do. Until the next post. Be comfy. Be chic. Mwaaaahs!

I submitted the diary to Anandi Ma'am the next day. I expected her to glance at it and return it to me. But she tucked it under her arm and said, 'I'll give it to you at the end of the day.' This happened every day of the week.

In this time, I wrote several cool-as-hell posts. And guess what? At the end of the fortnight, I couldn't help but notice that Anandi Ma'am had undergone a bit of a makeover herself!

End of week one, gone were the hideous flowers from her bun. The next week, out went the bun. And in the third week, she looked like a reasonably okay-looking teacher. Not like Sushmita in *Main Hoon Na*. Now that would be stretching it!

And was it my imagination or did she give my hand a little squeeze each time she handed the diary back to me?

Anyway, I went back to the blog and kept writing right up till the Pre-Boards. After that, the spectre of exams took over my life completely. ☹

Rinki Tripathi is taking an online quiz on Teenz Forever.

Online Quiz # 535. Self taught or Tutored: Do you need to take tuitions classes?

1. Your favourite subjects are:
    a. Gawd, I hate studying
    b. Accounts/Maths/Physics/Chemistry
2. Do you often find your attention wandering in class?
    a. Hey, how did you know?
    b. You're talking to Mr/Ms Mugpot, remember?

3. Have you ever been referred to as a 'teacher's pet'?
   a. Ha ha, whatte joke
   b. That is my middle name
4. Are you a good student?
   a. Refer to answer 1
   b. You bet!
5. Do grades matter?
   a. Only to my parents
   b. What kind of a question is this?

If you've scored mostly As: Trust us, you need tuitions. ASAP. In fact, don't even waste your time reading this. A good tutor will go a long way in improving your grades and maybe even instil a love for learning in you. Godspeed!

If you've scored mostly Bs: Hey, you don't need help. At least, not with your studies. You must have been through your, what, fifth revision, by now? Keep it up, future lawyer / scientist / doctor / engineer of the world. Too bad, the creative types don't see your true potential.

Rinki Tripathi scored mostly As.

Chapter 5

BlackBerry Messenger Status: Lord save me from Lord Gaga!

Okay, so it was decided. I was going to be sent to boot camp, aka Pragash Coaching Classes.

I felt like such a freak. I, who had pledged not to go anywhere near books (until the Boards were right around the corner), had ended up taking tuitions.

All my objections were swept aside heartlessly. My 'I'll study only at the 11th hour' resolve was crushed mercilessly. My valiant protests were no match for my parents' tyranny. And I was reduced to a tuition-taking minion. Tch tch! How the mighty had fallen.

And that was not the half of it. The tuition timings further rubbed salt on my wounds. An unearthly 6 a.m. to 7 a.m. Every Saturday and Sunday. Boooo hoooo.

Simple observation: Chennai is so full of early birds. In Delhi, if you happened to step out at six, you wouldn't see anyone. But I could be wrong. Maybe they were all out there, hidden under thick layers of smog. Anyway, in Chennai, restaurants are filled with people devouring idli-dosas;

'Suprabhatam' (classical wake-up song) is blaring out of music systems, people are jogging on the streets.

I had half a mind to rebel. I mean, think about it——

Taking tuitions: Baadddd

Having to wake up early on weekends for them: Sure and certain death!

Something like losing all your hair immediately after you've straightened *and* coloured it.

Turned out, I had a bigger problem waiting.

Anyway, the first day I almost ended up bunking class. Reason? No autorickshaw. I stood outside my apartment feeling much like an ornithologist waiting to catch sight of a rare migratory bird. A good half hour later, I was no closer to finding one.

One finally materialized. I did a quick arms-are-windmills-in-Holland dance for one whole minute, before he pretended to notice me.

'Village Road. How much?'

He pretended to carefully consider the destination. Then he raised all the five fingers of his left hand and made two zeroes with his right hand. '*Noor ruba.*'

Hundred bloody bucks!

'I said Village Road, not Vellore,' I muttered, my decibels rising along with my temper. 'Fifty, fifty rupees,' I signed, lifting five fingers and making one zero in the air.

He cocked an ear. 'Noor . . . hundred . . . rupiz. Not knowing Tamil, aa?'

Okay, here's the thing. In Delhi, if you hear something you don't like, you talk with your fists. But in Chennai, you merely thrust your right hand at someone. Like 'Crazy or what?' That's precisely what Auto Dude did before revving up the engine and zooming off.

'Poda, nai, panni,' I cursed after him, proving that I was familiar with the local lingo indeed.

Well, I'd no choice but to embark on my very own Dandi march. ('Morning walks are good for you,' Mausiji said when I cribbed to Mom later in the day. Yeah, right. So are menstrual cramps.)

I kept walking and walking till I reached an imposing wrought iron gate. I pushed at the door and a long driveway came into sight. There was a long line of tables right in the driveway. And there sat very many 'curd-rice cases', glasses firmly perched on their noses. (Curd-rice cases as in studious types).

I had half a mind to say, 'Oops, wrong address', turn tail and run out of there.

I took a couple of awkward steps towards the tables and peered at the students. Amazingly, they all looked alike. Where was, as they said in *Chak De India,* Coach Sir?

'Saar is et to come,' said a young mind reader, his hair neatly oiled and patted in place.

'You must be Rinkhee,' a voice boomed suddenly. It sounded like a mini bomb had gone off somewhere close by.

I spun around abruptly and nearly lost my balance. Not because of the sudden movement, but at the spectacle in front of me.

Remember Hagrid from Harry Potter? Pragash Sir looked like him. Only less groomed.

'Prakash, Sir . . .' I began.

'It's Pra-gash—ga, ga,' he corrected me. 'I see you're all puff and pant, Rinkhee. Came walking aaa?'

I nodded.

'Of course! You're so very engg, after all.'

'Engg'? After a second, realization dawned. Ah, he meant 'young'!

I could feel everyone's eyes on me. My ears turned red.

'Shy is coming, aaa?' Lord Gaga said with a laugh. 'Hmm, now where do I put Rinkhee? Next to Jerkis?'

'It's Xerxes, Sir,' pat came the reply from the first table.

'Or next to Hema, my favourite Tampon.'

WTF! I nearly choked before realizing he meant 'Tam Ponnu'. As in, Tamilian Girl.

Whew!

'Where, where, where . . .' Lord Gaga mused, eyeing the spot next to him.

Anywhere but there, I prayed silently.

'There's place here, Sir,' a heaven-sent voice piped up at the back.

Gosh, I really wanted to lift my skirt, go bouncing up to the voice and kiss its source.

There he was, this boy. Cute in a nerdy sort of way. (Who said nerds can't be cute? Just watch *The Big Bang Theory*; you'll know what I mean). Hmm. My saviour was skinny, had wavy brown hair that framed his solemn face and the kindest brown eyes.

I plonked myself next to him. Mouthed a heartfelt 'thanks'. He coughed in response.

Tuition class got underway. Lord Gaga rambled on and on. I tuned out completely.

I was thinking of Zara's spring—summer collection when Lord Gaga clapped his hands.

'Time forre surprise test. Let's see how smartiz you all are,' he chuckled.

Pointless exercise, if you ask me. If we were smart, would we really need tuitions?

Life's Greatest Mystery #5: Why do adults act first and think later (or not at all)?

I was totally unprepared. And that was the understatement of the year. I turned to my right. A guy in thick glasses hurriedly covered his answer sheet. A bookworm called Ravi. The cheapster! As if I would copy from him.

I mean, I would. Totally. But I wouldn't make it that obvious. I would pretend to look this way and that. Then slyly sneak a peek at his sheet. Like a pro, you know. Hey, I'd plenty of practice there. How do you think I cleared surprise tests back in Delhi?

But Ravi's paws completely covered his answer sheet from view. I was about to panic when Nerdy coughed. I swung my face around to look at him. He took his hand ever so slightly off his sheet, giving me a clear view. I flashed him a 100-watt smile in gratitude. He really was a SWEETIE PIE. If only he smiled more often. BTW, I also happened to see his name on the answer sheet. Adit.

After class, I sauntered up to him. 'Hey Adit, you going home?' I asked casually.

Adit nodded. 'You?'

'I don't know. Waiting for the Hogwarts Express to pick me up, I guess,' I joked.

He looked at me blankly.

Oh, for god's sake.

'I don't read *Harry Potter*,' he said, by way of explanation.

'That explains it then,' I said with a straight face. 'Yeah, so, I'll get going. God, I hate to walk, but guess all the walking will help me lose weight.'

'You don't need to lose weight,' Adit said indignantly.

I mean, I was instantly suspicious. Was he making fun of me? But no, there was not a flicker of sarcasm in his eyes. Not the slightest.

Gosh, I was totally floored. He meant it. He actually meant it. Yay! Someone had said I was thin. And I didn't even have to bribe/threaten/brainwash him.

'Why don't I drop you home?'

'Don't worry, I'm very "engg". I'll manage,' I quipped, wiggling my fingers to gesture 'walk'.

'No, no, I'll drop you.'

I shrugged and followed him down the road. He stopped abruptly next to a pink Scooty. I nearly choked.

'Don't tell me that's yours.'

'Fine, I won't,' he shrugged.

I waited patiently for a sane explanation.

'It's my sister's. Though I end up using it more often than her.'

'So it *is* your bike!' I exclaimed.

But by then he'd pulled his helmet on. Sigh. I had a knack for attracting (hey, not that 'attract'. Strictly in a manner of speaking) straight arrows in my life.

From Chennai Super Chick's Blog

People,

Any of you taking tuitions? Then you need these tips, URGENTLY. Don't go making all those blunders. Take it from me, they are tough to live down.

Disclaimer: The stuff in the 'Don't' section?——most of it is from imagination. Realllly. Promise. I swear.

Do	Don't
Pay attention to Sir / Ma'am	Think of the cute guy sitting next to you
Your homework	Copy it from the cute guy once you reach class
Reach class on time	Run in panting half an hour late
Sit in the back row	Sit right under tutor's nose
Starve	Eat before class is officially over (I'm sure they'll have a bell or something)
Drink water before class starts	Drink water mid-way, spilling it over your notes
Find out how much the fee is	Ask in a stage whisper, 'What are the damages?'
Talk before and after class	Discuss the late-night movie on HBO
Attend regularly	Bunk regularly
Raise your hand in time of doubt	Scream, 'One sec, one sec, didn't get that.'
Wear loose-fitting clothes	Wear tight tees and skinny jeans
Scrub your face clean	Wear loud make-up

Chapter 6

BlackBerry Messenger Status: And the Bickering Sisters Award goes to . . .

Are you tuned into Bigg Boss? Or Big Brother? Or any of those reality shows where people screech at the top of their lungs for no apparent reason? Have you watched a debate on Times Now? Where the anchor and the politician scream at each other at the same time?

Good, then you know what I'm talking about.

With Dad away in Coimbatore, Mom and Mausiji were driving me up the wall. And it was worse than Mom and Dad fighting. Or 'disagreeing', as my dad loved to put it. Really, I couldn't wait for Dad to wrap up this assignment, come back home and start his 'disagreements' with Mom all over again. That was so much better. Though I was expected to take sides ever so often, no one held any grudges. And we glided smoothly until the next shouting match.

No such luck with Mom and Mausiji. Gosh, they spared no opportunity to spar with each other! And they fought over the randomest of things. If I happened to be around, they'd look at me, ferocious dogs silently willing the hapless bone to settle matters.

At times, I'd have no choice but to play peacekeeper. But trust me, I had better things to do in life. For one thing, it really put me in a spot. For another, it totally drained me out. It was like being locked up in the Bigg Boss house for real. At least, the reel life inmates have sane families waiting outside. I couldn't even lay claim to that.

Too bad, the warriors were in no mood to back down.

I felt I had aged more in the last few months than in the last seventeen years. Instead of the wet-behind-the-years-teen, I feel like a wise-beyond-my-ears hag. Pity, India didn't have social security measures that removed young, impressionable minds from violent vicinities. Some serious rescuing was needed here.

Dad was in town the next weekend. And weekends with Dad around were C-R-A-Z-Y. Not the usual Tripathi household crazy. Ten thousand times worse. 'Run-because-the-devil-is-after-your-ass' crazy. Believe me.

The first weekend kind of set the tone. You know how our politicians act when the President of the US visits? Or how our socialites behave when Oprah Winfrey is in town? Well, that's how Mausiji behaved all through. She went all out in the kitchen.

Fact 1: Mausiji loved to cook.

Fact 2: Mom hated to. But what she hated even more was Mausiji walking away with brownie points. Especially on the weekends Dad was down.

That crucial weekend, Mausiji whipped up all of Dad's

favourite dishes—puris, aloo dum, kheer and what not. Needless to say, her enthu act didn't go down too well with Mom.

She held on to her temper with admirable restraint. And lost it only when she saw Dad acting like the leader of the Hungry Hordes.

'You're acting as if you don't get food in Coimbatore,' Mom remarked acerbically as Dad wolfed down yet another puri.

'Nothingsch comparedch tosh homesch madesch foodsch,' he slurped.

'Nothing compared to homemade food,' I translated dutifully.

'Are you feeling all right? That was your fifth puri.'

'Tch, tch,' Mausiji clucked. 'You better not count the number of puris the poor boy's eating.'

Mom shot Dad a look that said, 'You better start counting your days.'

Unable to stomach more of the saas-bahu drama, I gobbled down my food and made a beeline for my room.

I was passing by my parents' room when I heard raised voices. As if pulled by some magnetic force, my ear flew to the door. And stayed there.

(Important Note: A teenager needs to keep his/her eyes and ears open at all times. Vinita, my classmate back in Delhi, went through a harrowing time during her parents' divorce. You see, she was the last to know they were splitting. It was really hard on her. I'd sworn then and there to be always on the alert. If there ever would be trouble in paradise, I'd sniff it out right away. Oh, yeah.)

'I've been cooped up at home for weeks. I want to go out. Let's go pardy-shardy,' Mom whined. The TV volume went low.

'I can't remember the last time we did that,' Dad muttered. The TV volume went up.

'All you want to do is watch TV,' Mom cribbed. The TV volume went down.

'Sheena, please. I'm trying to relax.' The TV volume went up.

'Trust me, once you step out in the fresh air, you will relax,' Mom said cajolingly. The TV volume went down.

'Fresh air?' Dad said mockingly. 'There is only pollution outside.'

'Please, jaanu. Just put on your nice party shirt. We'll have fun. Just like old times.'

I heard a loud smack. Grrrrosssssssssssssssss!

That was all the inspiration I needed. I hastily removed my ear from their door.

When Mom came out of the room ten minutes later, she was decked in a put-your-sunglasses-on bright fuchsia salwar kameez. Gold jewellery adorned her ears and wrists.

Ladies and gentlemen, my mom. The Brand Ambassador of Bling!

'Going to pardy-shardy?' I couldn't resist asking.

'Night show, ' Mom said brightly. 'I wanted to go for dinner but Dad insisted we catch a movie.'

Dad and movie? That was like a cannibal opting for a vegetarian thali. And then it struck me. He wanted to catch a few zzzzs in the air-conditioned comforts of the theatre.

Mom gave me a tight hug when we heard Mausiji cough behind us.

'So, what time is the show? We don't want to be late, you know.' We turned around to find Mausiji all dolled up. Fire-engine red salwar kameez, matching-matching shoes and bag, heavily made-up eyes, vampire red lips.

Move over, Mom. You've got competition!

With the Band Bajaa Baraat out of the way, I could finally do my own thing. I BBMed Ankita, my BFF back in Delhi.

'Babes! What's up?' she typed back. A furious burst of smileys appeared on screen.

'Nothing much, yaar. Just vetti,' I typed back.

'Whatttt??'

'Sorry! "Vetti" as in "vela". Tamil slang for "jobless".

'My, my, someone has got a Masters in Tamil and all,' Ankita needled back.

'Far from it, da. My Tamil sucks.'

It was true. Kind of. While I did have an MCW (Master of Cuss Words degree), I could hardly string a few sentences together. Not without looking extremely self-conscious.

'Leave all that aside. Tell me what have you been doing? Have you met anyone? Any interesting guys around?'

'Boys, boys, boys! Is that all you can think of?' I retorted in mock irritation.

'No, I can also think of men.'

'Anks!'

'No, really. I'm seeing this really hot dude from St Stephen's College. He looks like Virat Kohli.' Ankita broke the news.

'The guy in those Fastrack ads?'

'The guy in those cricket matches. Seriously, Rinki. Don't you ever read the paper?'

'Sure I do.'

Ahem. Actually, there *were* a few sections of the paper I skipped. Occasionally. The front page, the sports page, the editorial and the international section. But I simply luuuurved the supplements. Newspaper supplements are like those mini idlis sprinkled liberally with red chilly powder. That's where you get all the masala from.

It was forever a bone of contention with Dad. Sigh. He wanted us, that's Mom and moi, to read the 'useful bits' of the paper every day.

I mean, can you imagine . . . Road accidents, politicians' speeches, death, murder, crime. Next day, repeat.

Anyway, with Dad away in Coimbatore, we were running free. In fact, Mom was even considering cancelling the newspaper subscription for the next few months.

'So tell me about your V. Kohli lookalike, Anks,' I asked, all interested.

'Now you're making him sound like that bacteria.'

'What bacteria?'

'You know, the one we learned about in VIII grade, E. Coli?' Ankita replied.

'Er, never mind, Anks. So you were saying . . .'

'Yeah, so, he is six feet tall, very fair, loves travelling, has a great voice and loves eating golgappas.'

'Sounds too good to be true,' I said, truly amazed. My friend had this knack of getting the best guys in the city.

I think it was partly because of her that I couldn't get any good guys to date. They were all taken. And tossed by her. I very well couldn't start dating the X-Men. If you know what I mean.

'Enough about me. What about you? Any cute guys in the picture?'

'Nah,' I replied, quickly. Too quickly.

'I know you better than that, Rinks. Out with it.'

'Well, I made friends with these two guys.'

'Two guys? Aren't you a fast chick!' Ankita marvelled.

'It's not what you think,' I protested.

'Explain! Now!'

'Okay, see, the first guy is Google . . .'

'Google? What sort of a name is that?'

'It's perfect for him, actually,' I typed.

'Good looking?'

'Umm, he's a bit on the chubbier side . . .'

'Okay, I've lost interest already. Moving on. Tell me about the parallel lead,' she commanded.

'Parallel lead? Heyllooooo, this is my life we're talking about and not some Bollywood masala flick!'

'Same diff,' Anks replied. 'The other guy. What's his name?'

The other guy? This was soooo not going in the right direction.

'Yeah, so, his name is Adit.'

'Short for?'

'Nothing. Just Adit.'

'So, is he into you?'

'More into books.'

'Rinks, are you seeing this guy or not?'

'Am not.'

'Then why are we having this conversation?'

Because I'm crazy enough to take you into confidence, I sighed to myself.

'Anyway, Rinks, chuck all this. Tell me, did you try that new gloss from MAC?'

And we moved on to a far more interesting topic.

I was late for tuitions. Again.

Pragash Sir looked none too pleased about it.

'Sorry, Sir, I forgot to set the alarm,' I panted from the exertion of running up the driveway.

He looked me up and down. 'Did you forjet to have breakfast, also?'

'No, Sir. I cannot study on an empty stomach,' I mumbled.

'Oho! So you come here to study, aa? I thaaat aal of you come here to havve gala time.'

'Noooooo, Sir,' the entire class chorused dutifully.

Gala time? At tuitions? That was like expecting Prince William to propose to me the day I got married to Prince Harry. Too far-fetched.

'Do naat be to say "No, Saar," when you do naat mean eet,' Pragash Sir thundered. 'You peoples, very worst.'

Hoo, boy. I was the one who was late but he was taking it out on the whole class. Not that I was complaining.

'You, you, you,' he stabbed his hairy finger in different directions. 'Come sit next to me.'

I sauntered up to Adit.

'Rinki, Sir pointed at you too,' he said gently.

Nooooooooooo! I possibly couldn't sit next to Pragash Sir. He was one of those people who thought showers had to be taken only on a weekly basis. Who thought personal grooming was for the birds. Who thought cleanliness was next to sadliness.

'Rinkhee, do you needde special invitation?'

No. But clearly, he needed a deodorant, a breath freshener and a lesson in personal hygiene.

'As punishment, you gette surprise test.'

Everyone groaned. I used the time wisely instead. Glued my eyes to my neighbour's notebook. Oh, hell. She was like the Beethoven of Accounts. Her fingers were practically flying over the black figures. She was arranging them like a beautiful symphony.

I'd such a hard time catching up. I wasn't even halfway through when she shut her notebook with a decisive *snap*!

Damn.

There was little else I could do. So I started doodling the gorgeous Mango gown I'd seen online the night before.

Pragash Sir cleared his throat.

'Time izze up. Let us see whaaat you've come up with . . . Rinkhee, show me.'

Oh god, no! This couldn't be happening.

Pragash Sir bent forward in slow motion and picked up my notebook.

Oh, no.

He'd almost brought it to eye level, when a low flying pigeon startled us all with its presence.

'Shoo, shoo, shoo, pinjun,' Pragash Sir hooted in a bid to scare it away.

Well, scared away it was. But not before it generously deposited his blessings on Sir's hand and my notebook.

'My haaand,' Sir cried out.

'My balance sheet,' I cried in relief, noting the tell-tale white blotch on the page.

I just loooooove the great outdoors, don't you?

Sir clutched his hand like it was diseased, and ran inside the house.

Adit rushed up to me. 'Are you okay?'

'Never been better.'

'I think class is cancelled,' Adit noted grimly.

You bet.

'So, Adit, what're you doing this evening?'

'Nothing. I'm vetti.'

'Join me at the Backyard?'

Now, Google's apartment had this lovely terrace. That's where we hung out. We called it the Backyard. All our bitching, bingeing, boozing sessions took place there. Uninterrupted.

Asking Adit to join us. That was mistake #1.

Really. It was all downhill after that.

Google greeted Adit with a loud, 'Hi, Bromo.'

'Bromo?' Adit asked, puzzled.

'A brother who's a homo,' I said without thinking. Mistake #2.

Google proceeded to fix Adit a glass of rum. That was like offering the Pope an AK-47. The cover of Chetan Bhagat's *The Three Mistakes of My Life* popped into my head.

'Hey, cheers!' Google said with a flourish.

'I don't drink,' Mr Goody Two-shoes replied.

'Okay, how about a fag then?'

'I don't smoke,' Adit said curtly.

'You don't have tea also? Lactose intolerant or what?'

Adit flashed me a look that said, 'Is he on dope or what?'

I shot him a look that said, 'He's like that only. Don't mind.'

Google ignored the glacial expression on Adit's face and poured a large rum for himself.

Unfortunately, Robin couldn't make it that evening. Sriram was going away to Manipal for his MBA course. So naturally, the couple wanted to spend some 'alone' time together. Thank god for Sudha. I was happy to have company during the Ice Ages.

BTW, did I mention, Sudha was besotted with Google? I mean, totally.

Remember the scene from *Main Hoon Na*? Where SRK sees violinists, singers, the full orchestra when he sets sights on Sushmita? The same thing happened to Sudha each time she set eyes on Google. Except in her head she saw guys with mridangams and veenas, being the traditional girl she is.

Google, however, couldn't care less about Sudha.

'I wish Robin and Sriram were here,' I sighed. 'Here's to love.'

'Don't worry, Rinki. It'll happen to you, too,' Google, who appeared to be on a liquid diet (three large rums and counting), clucked in sympathy.

'I'm not worried,' I said quickly. A little too quickly. Gawd. I was embarrassed. Googs was talking rubbish. In front of our new friend, of all people. I didn't want Adit to think I was a despo. Because, obvs, I was NOT.

'You should lower your standards, you know. You keep thinking that a handsome prince will come and sweep you off your feet.'

'Of course not,' I denied hotly.

Of course, I wanted Prince Charming to sweep me off my feet. I mean, who didn't? I was so looking forward to Mr Right: A sensitive, caring, sweet, funny, intelligent guy. Who was the right height, the right weight, the right complexion. I'd drawn up a list and . . .

'But why will a handsome prince go for someone like you?' Google cut into my thoughts.

'Why not? What's so wrong with me?' I asked indignantly, my voice shrill.

Adit was gorging on the paneer tikkas as if all the dairies in Chennai were going on strike the next day.

'Aha, so you admit there's something wrong with you! Thanks for proving my theory correct.'

'Shuddup, Googs,' I hissed. Gosh, he was annoying.

'Don't get me wrong, Rinks. Think practically. Will you go in for someone who is ugly, dumb and clumsy? You'll want someone of your standard. At least.'

A giggle escaped Sudha.

Oh, funny, was it?

'I just want a normal guy who treats me well, keeps himself clean and has something between his ears. Is that too much to ask?' I sniffed.

'Afraid so,' said Google, his head bobbing up and down. 'By treating you well, you mean having marathon "emo" conversations.'

'What's "emo"?' Adit wanted to know.

'Dude, "emo" as in "emotional". Like that Edward creature in *Twilight*. And that movie *Breaking Dawn*, yuck! Piece of crap, if you ask me.'

Ommmmgggggg, this was blasphemy! The whole world and its wife knew that I was a Twihard—a die-hard *Twilight* fan. Plus, *Breaking Dawn* was my favouritist movie in the franchise. It'd got everything a girl could ask for. In reel life and real: Dreamy dude. Romance. Love. Marriage. Honeymoon. Make-out scenes.

'Guys are more into action, you know,' Google Express was rambling on. 'Oh, yeah! They don't like to sit around talking about the next waxing appointment, nail paint . . . all that silly chick stuff.'

'You mean, *you* don't like to. And duuuude, what're you gabbing on about? You don't even have a girlfriend,' I countered spiritedly.

'Trust me, if I had one, I wouldn't tag along everywhere with her. You tell me, Adit, would you go with your GF for her waxing session?'

'Sure, I would,' Adit said, taking all of us by surprise.

Awwww.

'Soooo sweet,' Sudha and I chimed in.

'Give me a break, dude,' Google gagged.

'I mean it,' Adit said, his brown eyes serious.

'Ooooh, what do we have here?' Google hollered. 'A SNAG, are you?'

'SNAG?' Adit asked the question, but all of us wanted to know the answer.

'Sensitive New Age Guy,' Google chortled.

Adit rolled his eyes.

'Well, the girls are going to the parlour tomorrow. Why don't you tag along with them?' Google challenged him.

'It's not the same thing,' I protested mildly. 'He said he'd accompany his *girlfriend*, Google.'

'Sudha and Rinki are friends. AND they are girls. Suds, Rinks, correct me if I'm wrong.'

I stuck my tongue out at him. Adit merely shook his head. 'Not for a million bucks.'

'I just knew it! I knew he wouldn't go. It takes a real man to keep his word,' said Google.

'I'm a real man,' said Adit defensively.

'Prove it,' said Google calmly.

'What do you mean "prove it"?'

Sudha covered her eyes in terror.

'Go. Parlour. Tomorrow.'

Adit stood transfixed, as if he couldn't digest the request.

'Adit is a sissy, Adit is a sissy,' sang Google in his most irritating baby-voice.

'Oh, shut up, Googs. You're blabbering. No one's going to the parlour,' I declared. 'Except me. It's time for my monthly beauty session. Manicure, pedicure, hair spa and fruit facial.' I ticked off my fingers.

'Wow! You do all *that* and still look like *this*,' Google said in genuine amazement.

I threw a piece of chicken tikka at him.

From Chennai Super Chick's Blog

Okay, be honest now. What's the first thing you notice in a guy?

His eyes?

His smile?

His hair?

His clothes?

His confidence?

Any other . . .

Mail me quick.

And if you're a guy and happen to be reading this, don't worry. Reading a fashion blog is nothing to be ashamed of. Everyone needs a dose of style. We're in the 21st century, for god's sake.

What's the first thing you notice in a girl?

Her eyes?

Her smile?

Her hair?

Her figure?

Her clothes?

Her confidence?

Any other . . .

Okay, here's what I think.

I think most girls notice a guy's face. So it's best to keep it clean.

A straggly moustache is so not on. It looks artificial and makes you look like spring chicken.

Ditto for beard. Unless you are Robert Pattinson. Anything goes then. No questions asked.

Long curls are passé. Good thing too. Think maintenance. Think lustrous locks. Think less expenditure on shampoos.

Consider investing in a good conditioner. Leave it or wash out. Groomed hair DOES NOT make a wimp. On the contrary, it makes you super cool and date-able.

Also, do not step out without dousing yourself with deo. India is a tropical country. Translation: we tend to sweat. A lot. You can't go wrong with a deo. Perfume is good too. Nothing fruity or floral, puhleese.

Last but not the least: If you're going on a date, please remember to brush your teeth. And/or chomp on a gum stick. Can't be lax about this one.

As for my dear chicas, please follow all the above pointers.

Yup, including the ones on the moustache and the beard. Especially the ones on the moustache and the beard.

Hit the parlour once in two weeks to get rid of the fuzzy growth above and below your mouth. Trust me, it can be very distracting during a conversation.

Waxing/shaving/epilators are also a must-do. Subject to how fast your hair grows.

And invest in a good haircut. One that frames your face. Complements your personality. It goes a long way in making you look like a true-blue styloo. Which is what you aspire to be, righto??

Till my next post, laulies!

Mwaaaahs!

Chapter 7

BlackBerry Messenger Status: Your greatest fear shall come true.

It's a universal truth, my BBM status. Right up there with 'The #$%^ will hit the fan', 'What goes up will hurtle down at breakneck speed', 'If something has to go wrong, it sure as hell will'.

Not sure who said all the above. But whoever did was a Genius.

Take my biggest fear, for instance. No, no, it was not:

1. Getting caught red-handed by my parents
2. Flunking the Board Exams
3. Coming to school in my birthday suit (Oh, but, wait, that was my favourite nightmare. Yes, there's a difference between the two)
4. Waking up in a boy's body (Eww!)

It was something far, far more complex: Being summoned to our Princy, Mrs Verghese's, cabin. Really. It's right up there with all those phobias. I'd even coined a name for it. Verghese-itis.

Each time I got the summons, I developed all the symptoms. In a heartbeat. My mouth went dry, my heart started beating a wild tango, my knuckles went white, my hands went cold, my legs felt lifeless.

Usually, XI and XII graders were summoned for a severe tongue-lashing (during report card distribution) or when some crime (crackers in loo variety) had been committed. It was never, ever for a good cause.

And I was not being pessimistic. In the last one year, Mrs Verghese had called people only to berate them for something they had or hadn't done. So, when her peon came calling for me in the month of September, I was caught off guard.

Between school and tuitions (not to mention, between Mom and Mausiji), I hardly had the time to get into trouble. I ran a mental checklist of my activities in the last one month. Nothing there. I'd kept my nose out of trouble indeed.

Trouble was, I'd also kept my nose out of books. But Term Exams were two months away. No, it couldn't be anything academic. So, what could it be?

Hey, have you seen the movie *The Green Mile?* It's the distance a prisoner walks from his cell to the gallows. And as I dragged my feet to Mrs Verghese's cabin, I felt I was doing the exact same thing. Only difference, I was already dead by the time I reached the execution area.

I wiped my damp hands on my kameez and proceeded to knock on the door. Kameez. Yes, you heard me right. That's what our school uniform was at Chennai Bal Vidya Bhawan.

'Come in,' Princy said, her tones decidedly (and worryingly) frosty.

I pushed the door open and stood rooted to the spot.

'Do you need a formal invitation to walk to the chair?'

That galvanized me into action. I stumbled towards her table, almost tripping over myself.

'Sit,' she barked.

'How are the collections for "Help the Elderly" coming along?'

I mumbled something unintelligible, then finally let out the breath I was holding. It wasn't anything sinister. It was just a routine enquiry. Last month, Anandi Ma'am had asked us to collect donations for 'Help the Elderly.'

I had collected, what, two hundred and fifty rupees in the last few weeks. I wasn't exactly proud of the sum but hey, there was nothing much I could do. People aren't very generous when it comes to this sort of a thing. I mean, would you trust a teenager with a chanda box? For all you know, she'd spend it on booze or fags or something worse.

'Your father works at Citibank, doesn't he?'

'No,' I said hastily.

She raised an eyebrow.

'I mean, yes. Yes, he works at Citibank. But he's in Coimbatore at the moment.'

'Surely he can put in a word with his colleagues, friends, acquaintances. Shouldn't be too difficult for you to get five thousand rupees?'

It wasn't a question.

Forget five grand, it'd be difficult for me to collect fifty bucks. Of course, I didn't tell her that.

I felt damn uncomfy asking people for things, let alone money. And asking my dad to ask his colleagues? Out of the question! Why didn't she just place a bowl in my hand and send me to a traffic signal?

'Two weeks should do.'

Again, it was a not a question.

I smiled weakly.

She went back to her papers. And I went back to my dark thoughts.

As I walked into the living room with a long face, Mom looked up and did a double take upon seeing my woebegone expression.

'Rinki, what happened? Are you okay?'

She hurried over to me and placed her palm on my forehead. This was something Mom had been doing ever since my childhood. Whenever she saw something amiss, she would start checking if I had fever. Don't ask.

'Mom, please. I am fine. Don't worry.'

'Sure? You look stressed . . .'

Tell me about it, Mom.

'. . . and tired.'

Not to mention old. Haggard, even.

Mausiji spoke up. 'What else can you expect when she diets all the time?'

Me and diet?! Anyone who knew Rinki Tripathi knew that the word didn't exist in her lexicon. Sure, I'd like to be skinny, but I wouldn't give up food for that. No chance in hell!

I decided to ignore her. I'd had enough of one dementor back at school. I couldn't handle another one.

Suddenly I had a brainwave. 'Mom, I'm collecting donations for this home for senior citizens. Would you like to contribute?'

'I did contribute. Last month, remember? I gave you fifty rupees.'

Damn, she remembered. Sob. In this day and age, who contributes fifty bucks? Even those balloons on Marina Beach cost more.

'Oh, sorry, I forgot. I mean, you could always donate some more? Think of all those poor souls. They will get to live better and bless you for all your help.' I broke off and looked at Mausiji meaningfully.

She refused to meet my gaze. I half expected her to melt like a firangi IPL player in Chennai's heat. But Mausiji was one tough nut.

Hmm, I'd have to think of something else. But days turned to weeks and my collections didn't go up by more than a hundred measly bucks. Dreading another bout of Verghese-itis, I went in for the inevitable. I broke open my piggy bank. I counted all the dough I'd been saving for my hair straightening job (sob, sob, sob), and decided to part with it for a noble cause. Youngistan sacrificed for senior citizens.

It was more important to have hair on the head. Gorgeous hair could wait.

From Chennai Super Chick's Blog

Heylooo!

Please answer the following questions and see if this post is meant for you.

Are you obsessed with your weight?

Are you shy/shamed/embarrassed discussing your weight in public?

Do you see the weighing scale more often than your family and friends?

Do you avoid making friends with people skinnier than you?

Do you always volunteer to click the photograph when you're in a group?

Do your (rare) photographs make you cringe?

If you could change one thing about yourself, would it be (ha ha, no-brainer) your weight?

Do you ever fantasize about going to sleep and waking up five/ten/more kgs lighter?

If you've answered yes to any four of the above questions, congrats. This post is dedicated to you. Rest of you lucky bums, I hate you!

Kidding. Kind of.

Confession: I'm weight-challenged. Hence, this post.

Now if you've been fighting the Battle of the Bulge (and losing consistently), all is not lost. Pardon the pun.

It's a universally accepted fact: Some of us are blessed with good metabolism. The rest of us are screwed.

So, if you belong to the latter category, you need to do more than just fret and fume.

You need to exercise. Or so I was told. Well, I tried it. Briefly. And when that didn't work, I did the next best thing. I read self-help books by dieticians, formerly weight-challenged celebrities and yoga gurus.

After weeks of reading and researching, I reached a sad conclusion.

You can exercise all you want, but unless you control your diet, those fat cells aren't going anywhere.

And that's a major problem for me. I HAAAATE that diet word from the bottom of my heavy bottom.

Which brings me back to the perennial problem. How the hell do I lose weight?

Any ideas, suggestions, thoughts? Write to me ASAP.

Toodles!

Xoxoxo

CSC

Chapter 8

BlackBerry Messenger Status: Of Babes and Behenjis!

My non-existent love life suddenly registered signs of activity. As if all that drama on the home and school front wasn't enough.

Crazzzyyy with a capital C, the way it happened. One minute, Googs and I were clinking our beer mugs at the Backyard, and the next, he was asking me out!

'Everyone's ditched us,' Google began dramatically. 'Robin and Sriram . . .'

'You don't even know Sriram. You've only heard of the guy,' I interrupted.

'. . . Neha and Sudha,' Google continued morosely. 'I guess everyone has better things to do on a Saturday night . . .'

'Than hang out with a bunch of losers,' I completed. 'Let's drink to that. Cheers!'

Google slammed down his beer mug. 'Rinki, I was just thinking, hic.'

'You? Thinking? Interesting,' I said teasingly.

'What?' Google growled. 'I'm not intellectual enough for you? Hic-hic.'

'You're not intellectual enough for anyone. You're not an intellectual. Period,' I replied in all earnestness.

'A-a-and, hic, that sissy Adit of yours?'

'He's not a sissy,' I snapped without thinking. 'And he's not my Adit,' I hastened to add.

'Well, hic, he reminds me of someone. All that seriousness, all that let's-talk-about-our-feelings stuff. Who's that dude you dig? Eddie Weddie something.'

He. Did. Not. Mean. Edward. MY EDWARD. Of *Twilight* fame.

That set me thinking. Was Google right? Was Adit remotely like Edward? Sure, he was sweet and sensitive, but but but. . . .

'Know the problem with those guys?' Google Baba continued dispensing gems of relationship wisdom. 'They don't want to hang out with dumb chicks. They want to be around like-minded nerdy types—clad in kurtas, jholas, chappals.'

'That's such a cliché, Google,' I pooh-poohed out loud.

I sure as hell didn't believe it. But what if I were wrong? Worse, what if Google was right? What if all the smart guys wanted uncool chicks? Where would that leave girls like me? Saddled with a long line of losers. Shudder!

'Think about it, hic, Rinki. If a girl spends all her time reading *Sunday Times*, *Shakespeare* and science journals, hic, when would she find the time to read *Stardust*?'

A disturbing thought popped into my head. Just a while ago, I'd goaded Mom into cancelling our newspaper subscription. Gawd. I wanted to weep.

Google continued, unabashed, 'Hmm. I can tell if a girl's a dumbo or nerdy just by looking at her nails. Long and painted—dumbo. Bitten off and badly kept—nerdy.'

The double coat of Maybelline on my nails flashed accusingly in the dark. I quickly stuffed my hands into the back pockets of my jeans.

'Google, shudduup! As if there are only two types of chicks in the world! You aren't making any sense.'

'Rinks, I know that you know that I'm talking sense. Hic, hic. Hear me out, please. I've a proposition for you.'

Nooooo, not a proposition. Anything but a proposition.

'You could wait and wait for your Santa Claus . . .'

'Santa Claus?' I butted in.

'You know, the guy who does not exist. Or you could go out with someone real. Someone like me. Hic. Take my advice, Rinki. Don't miss the bus.'

Wow. As proposals go, it was certainly out of the box.

Maybe he had a point. Maybe I got all jittery, maybe it was the vodka, but I found myself accepting.

Agreed, Google was no McDreamy. He wasn't the right height or the right weight or the right anything. He just didn't make it on The List. You know, the list of virtues a boy was required to possess to be considered my BF material.

But like the guy said, he was real. And he had asked me out. And it was not as if there were tons of boys beating my door down.

So there.

Actually, I was wayyy more nervous about other ground realities. I mean, there were lots of things to consider. My ridiculous 8 p.m. deadline, for instance. How on earth could I go on a date AND be back by 8 p.m.?

Important note: There was a funny debate on FB the other day. Apparently, the government wanted to raise the drinking age to twenty-five. Great! Just when I was going to turn eighteen. Add that to Chennai's ridiculous 10.30 p.m. deadline for the last order. Well, left to my parents, they'd keep it to 9 p.m. but let's not go there . . .

Why don't they just get together and kill us? Once and for all. I mean, what exactly are they getting at? Should we wait till we are old hags to get smashed? Really now. And then they wonder why alcoholism is a big problem among the youth.

All so silly. Such a colossal waste of time. Make someone young the PM, I say. Moi, for instance. Even for a day. That's all I need to set things right. Gosh, now I sound like my dad. Speaking of whom, I was actually missing the guy. Who would've thought! Well, he flew down most weekends. But for some reason or the other, I couldn't get to see much of him.

Anyway, back to the date. Google was bursting with ideas.

Google's Galatta Plan (Galatta=Hungama)

Part I: Plan the date for a weekend when I'd be home alone. Translation: Mom–Dad at the movies.

Part II: Slip 'something' in Mausiji's tea. It'd knock her out for sometime.

Part III: Arrange pillows on the bed (in case Mom–Dad got back early) and sneak out.

Sounded good, the plan. But there were several loopholes:

1. What if Mausiji woke up just in time to catch me? Red-handed?
2. What if Mausiji didn't wake up at all? What'd I do then? I'd be a murderer and Google an accomplice to crime.
3. What if Mom and Dad didn't go out next weekend? That was known to happen. What'd I do then?

I wanted to broach the topic with Mom. So, I did what I usually did under the circumstances. Played out the scenarios in my mind beforehand.

Silly Goose Scenario #1.
Rinki: Mom, I am going to Zara Tapas.
    Mom: Okay, but be back at 8.
    Rinki: Mom, Zara Tapas opens at 9.
    Mom: Okay, then call your friends home.

So Innocent Scenario #2.
Rinki: Mom, Robin's celebrating her birthday at Pizza Hut.
    Mom: Isn't it rather late for lunch?
    Rinki: She's buying us dinner, actually.
    Mom: Okay, then I'll give the maid the evening off. Parcel a pizza for me. Will ask Mausiji if she wants garlic bread. But be back by 8.

Smart Cookie Scenario #3.
Rinki: Mom, I've called the girls home for a sleepover.
    Mom: Okay, ask them to come after 8.30. I'll be done watching my serial by then.

Rinki: Sorry, no serial for you tonight. We'll be watching the IPLs. Great match tonight. Chennai Super Kings vs Delhi Daredevils.

Mom: Can't you have the sleepover at Robin's place?

See, it was that simple. I went with Scenario 3.

Mom reacted just the way I'd hoped. To be expected. Totally unexpected was Mausiji's reaction.

'Sheena, how can you allow a young girl to roam the streets at night?'

Wow, so I was a streetwalker now.

'Don't worry, Mausiji. This is not her first time.'

Mausiji raised a brow. It was just the way she lifted it, you know. As if she had totally sized up me, my character, Mom's parenting skills or the lack of it thereof.

'Not her first time? Hey Ram! Back in the day, mothers would guard their daughters with their life. Treat them like precious possessions, keep them under lock and key . . .'

Thank god I wasn't born back in the day.

'You expected nothing less from good families. And these days, mothers are escorting daughters to sin city. Tch tch, what has the world has come to?'

I suddenly had a vision. I was this aspiring actress, clad in a tube top and the tiniest of shorts, and Mom was accompanying me to a lecherous producer's office.

I wanted to throw my head back and laugh. Mom, on the other hand, was in no mood to laugh. I mean, I could see the crazy gleam in her eyes. Now those who know her well (Dad and I) know the gleam is a good time to back off. But Mausiji being Mausiji had no clue.

'You're sending all the wrong signals to the hungry wolves of the city. Sending your daughter out like that. I'm telling you,' she clucked.

Sin city, hungry wolves. Live Soap at Tripathi Villa, anyone?

'And I'm telling you that I'll do what I think is best for my daughter. Rinki, pack your overnight bag. I'll drop you to Robin's. Let's see who dares to mess with me!' thundered Mom.

If I were a hungry wolf and I saw *that* crazy gleam in Mom's eyes, I certainly wouldn't.

I ran to the room, my heart thumping. Dumped the first set of clothes I could lay my hands on into my rucksack, hoisted it on my shoulder. Within seconds, I was out of the door.

It was only when we reached the parking lot that we realized: we'd left the car keys back in the house.

There was deathly silence.

'I'm not going back up there,' Mom finally spoke up.

'What??'

'I want to come to Robin's house,' Mom muttered.

Oh, hell.

'M-mom, calm down. Please! Just take deep breaths. You cannot come over for a night stay. You know that.'

'Who says I can't?' she retorted. Her hair was whipping about in the wind, there was a deathly gleam in her eyes. It was eerie the way she reminded me of, well, me.

'Look, Mom, this is my sleepover, remember. Why don't we do this "Mom and I" outing some other time?' I pleaded.

Desperately trying to think of a plausible excuse, I snapped my fingers as a sudden inspiration struck me. 'We'll book ourselves into a nice hotel for a long weekend and let Mausiji mind the house. What say?'

For a moment there, I was worried that Mom wouldn't agree. A few tense seconds ticked by. Eventually, she flashed me a weak smile. 'Okay, let me drop you to Robin's.'

I threw my arms around her and gave her a big hug. With Mausiji around, I was actually rooting for my Mom. Who would've thought that the generation gap could actually set things right?

Google had parked his car down the road from Robin's house. Just to be on the safe side. I slid into the passenger seat, a big frown on my face.

'Hey, nice dress,' Google beamed.

That cheered me up instantly.

I'd chosen a black A-line dress (trust me, you just can't go wrong with black. It's so forgiving). It had long, lacy sleeves and a simple scooped neck. I'd paired it with black sheer leggings. The effect was simple and (even if I may say so myself) striking. Once in the car, I completed the look with minimum accessories—silver hoops, a slim watch and peep-toe slingbacks. Applause! Thank you. Nandri. Merci. Danke. Grazie.

'Thanks, Googs.'

'Music?'

'Sure! What kind of music are you into?'

'Bollywood. Is there any other kind?' Google wondered.

Hell, yeah.

Loud strains of *Bachna ae haseeno* filled the car.

'Girls, you stand warned,' Google bellowed.

I grinned at him. 'Where are we going?'

'Amethyst. Been there before?'

'No, Googs,' I said sarcastically. 'Until you came along, I was perfectly happy living under a rock.'

'What?' Google asked, puzzled.

Sigh.

'Never mind. Amethyst, here we come!'

Amethyst was awesome even in the evenings. There was a lot of greenery around. The trees were decorated with fairy lights. There was a flower shop selling exotic flowers, and a gorgeous store selling designer threads at exotic prices. The place was crawling with firangs. I felt as if I'd been transported somewhere abroad.

The date wasn't so bad either. Though is it technically a date if two people just hog and hog and hog without once looking up from their plates?

Except to rave:

'My apple—pineapple—orange…slurp…mocktail…slurp… is fab.'

'Wait till you take a sip of my . . . slurp . . . apple shake . . . slurp.'

'My chicken . . . chomp-chomp . . . pesto is great.'

'My tuna . . . chomp-chomp . . . sandwich is to die for.'

'Hey, Rinki, that was a giant bite. Get your own chocolate brownie.'

'It is my chocolate brownie. You ordered mango soufflé, remember?'

'Fine, Rinki, I'm sho shorry. Order another brownie. Wait, make that two!'

Trust me, it was like an Eatomania Contest. May the better contestant win. And the better contestant did win. Google polished off two chocolate brownies, after sharing mine.

Yeah, so, the only time Google looked up was to ask for the cheque. Which, by the way, he gallantly cleared.

I guess it was a date, after all.

After dinner, Google dropped me at Robin's place for the sleepover.

Sad truth: The last Mom vs Mausiji session was just a trailer. The worst was 'et to come'.

'Their upbringing's all wrong.' It all started with this one statement. Uttered by Mausiji early next day.

Did my phonathons with Ankita, Robin, Adit, Google and Sudha have something to do with it? Four hours, forty-five minutes and counting. (One hour fifteen minutes per person. Wasn't much, if you looked at it this way.)

As it happened that fateful day, the phone was dangling from my ear when Mausiji started her tirade.

Mom and Mausiji had been watching a soap on TV. The one that starred a bunch of teens. The hero's family had just discovered that he was an alcoholic. He was stealing precious stuff from home. Selling it at Chor Bazaar to buy his booze. Blah, blah.

'Tch tch,' Mausiji began. 'In my time, children were brought up to be mature, responsible adults . . .'

'Oh, yeah. Your nephew is a shining example,' Mom sneered.

'Now, now, Mom, there's no need to drag Dad into it,' I pitched in. Granted, Dad was nowhere near perfect. But he'd turned out okay. Well, sort of.

'What was that again, Rinks?' Robin's voice grated in my ear. She'd just had a minor tiff with Sriram and was making a big deal about it. I wanted her to get over it already. Fights happen. You scream, shout, clear your lungs and move on. She could have asked my family for tips, you know.

'Sorry, Robin, GTG. Family emergency,' I said abruptly. I hung up and padded across the room. The desi ninjas faced each other, hands on their wide hips, scowls on their ferocious faces.

'Guys, guys, stop it,' I said.

'Ask your mom to stop. She is the one who started it.'

'I did not.'

'You did!'

And suddenly I had a vision. There I was, playing Arnie's role in *Kindergarten Cop*. Only the entire kiddie cast had been annihilated by sword-wielding dwarves who looked suspiciously like Mom and Mausiji.

'Mom, Mausiji, puhlllllease! It doesn't matter who started it. Please stop fighting.'

'I was not fighting. I was just showing her the error of her ways,' Mom pouted, sitting down on the couch heavily.

'I wasn't fighting either. I was just telling her that kids these days are such brats. We did things differently. That's why our kids are so different.'

'Are you trying to say I haven't done a good job with Rinki?' Mom retaliated.

I personally thought Mom had done a phenomenal job. But before I could so much as take a bow, Mausiji interrupted.

'Good is the enemy of great.'

Clearly, Mausiji had been reading too many self-help books.

'Just hand over the responsibility to me and see,' she answered.

'Now, now . . .' I began.

'And what will you do? Wave a magic wand and make her perfect?' Mom cut in sharply.

Ouch! My mom didn't think her one and only kid, her flesh and blood, was perfect? She thought that she needed work? That she could be improved upon? For some reason, that really, really, really hurt. Weren't moms supposed to love their kids unconditionally? Warts and all? Weren't they supposed to turn a blind eye to their shortcomings and love them all the same? Or had I been reading the wrong books? Watching the wrong movies? Hanging out with the wrong folk?

'Two weeks. That's all I need. Give me two weeks. And see the wonders I work with her,' Mausiji boasted, a wide smile on her face.

As if I was some building in need of urgent renovation.

'All the best, Mausiji,' Mom said, settling down into the couch to watch the next prime-time soap.

'That's it, guys! I am so out of here.' With that, I stormed out of the room.

Not fast enough. Because I heard Mom crib, 'Why does she keep doing that?'

'And why does she keep calling us "guys"?' Mausiji added.

Week One of the Official Handover of Rinki to Mausiji, and all hell broke loose.

It was Saturday evening and I was all set to go on another date with Google. I popped my head into the kitchen to take stock of Mom's whereabouts. She was giving Rakamma a demo on The Right Way of Cleaning Utensils.

Precisely why I never volunteered to help Mom with household chores. Because she nitpicked and nagged and did everything all over again anyway.

'You wash utensils *romba romba* fast. Hold plate under the tap. Like this. Then, rotate it like this like this. Okay, va?'

'*Seri, seri*,' Rakamma nodded. And proceeded to do exactly what she'd been doing all these days.

Sigh.

'Bye Mom! Am off. See you at night.'

'Night? I thought your tuition class was postponed to six in the evening?' Mausiji, the self-appointed Sherlock Holmes of the household, spoke up.

'Yes, Mausiji. But the gang . . .' I replied patiently.

'Gang?' she gasped, her eyes bulging.

'My group of friends,' I amended hastily. 'We're going for early dinner after class.'

'Where?'

Duuuuh.

'To a restaurant.'

'Which restaurant?'

As if she knew all the restaurants in the city. As if she knew the difference between 'Murugan Idly Shop' and 'Velu Military Chicken'.

'Amethyst. It's this lovely coffee shop . . .'

'You just said dinner, now you're saying coffee shop,' Mausiji said suspiciously.

'It's where we hang,' I shrugged.

'Hang-shang?' Mausiji parroted, her eyes as big as saucers.

'You know, a cool place where they serve sandwiches and pastas and pizzas and . . .'

'No need to tell me the menu,' she said rudely.

'. . . Pastries,' I completed.

'How will you go there?'

Gawd, she was like this astronaut on a fact-finding mission.

'Well, I've asked for my private jet,' I said with a straight face. Her face was blank.

Sigh. 'Someone will get a car and drive us there,' I elucidated.

'Is that someone a girl?'

'Or so she claims,' I said, my tongue firmly lodged in my cheek.

Mausiji narrowed her eyes.

'Does she have a name? And more importantly, does she have a license?'

'Check, on both counts, Mausiji.'

'How old is she? How come she has a license?'

'Mera Bharat Mahaan, Mausiji,' I replied sweetly. Just not as mahaan as you, I added under my breath.

'Okey dokey, I'm getting late. So, if you'll excuse me, ladies, I've got to go. Byeeeee!'

I waved at them cheerfully and ran towards the door. I glanced down at my watch. Shoot, I was five minutes behind schedule. Google would be waiting below, hopping mad.

I jabbed at the elevator button. Nothing. Damn! It was stuck on some floor above. I could hear the mechanized voice entreating, 'Please shut the door'.

There was no time to be lost. So I did a Run Forrest Run. I scurried down the stairs and hurried out. Google had parked right next to the gate, earning the watchman's ire. Just great.

I scrambled into the car.

'What took you so long?' Google erupted.

'Good to see you too. Just a sec, let me check if I've got my wallet.'

I plunged my hand into my rucksack. We lost precious time digging.

In the meanwhile, who should turn up at the gate but Mausiji.

'Wait up!' she hollered.

Google craned his neck to get a good look at her. Gawd! She made a scary sight. What with her dyed hair flying all over her pale face, her sari flapping in the wind, her arms flailing about.

'Go, go, go!' I shrieked.

In his agitation, Google dropped the car keys on the floor.

Mausiji bounded up to the car and threw herself full force on the rear windshield. She lay there, spreadeagled, like Batman, panting for breath.

'What the #$%,' gasped Google as he retrieved the keys and thrust them in the ignition.

'Step on it,' I roared as the engine came to life.

We took off in a cloud of dust, Google swerving expertly to avoid the open ditch right outside my building.

I didn't expect Mausiji to give chase, but inexplicably she did. I craned my neck and POUFFF! One minute she was running after the car and the next, she was nowhere to be seen.

'#$%^! #$%^! #$$%!' screamed Google. 'She's fallen in, I think!'

What is with Chennai and all the digging, dude? I just don't get it. Summer, they dig. Monsoons, they dig. Winters, they dig some more. At any time of the year, they dig up the roads. And leave them like that for months on end. Bloody ditches. Waiting open-mouthed for trouble. It was in one such ditch that Mausiji found herself.

Google Search: Physiotherapists in Chennai
From Chennai Super Chick's Blog

Okay, I finally found it. A diet that lets you hog all you want and keeps you slim.

Now that's what I've been looking for all my life.

Shared by my friend A.

He got this book (yes, he likes to read) from his club library.

It's by some hotshot dietician.

She says we can eat all that we want.

All we've got to do is eat small, eat frequently and bingo, we can look like Kareena in Tashan.

Er, kind of.

Will check it out.

Until then, if you know of a reasonable, non-starving way to lose weight, do share.

And oh, no blood group diets, no Atkins, no fruit only, no-low-carb-high-protein diets.

They don't work. Not for me. Not that I've tried them. Nor do I ever intend to.

Am just saying.

Bye!

Xoxoxo

CSC

Chapter 9

BlackBerry Messenger Status: Sorry, Bhai!

After the Mausiji-falling-into-ditch fiasco happened, we almost welcomed a new member into our family.

See, I'd lied to Mom and she confronted me later that night. I walked in to find Mausiji rubbing Iodex on her ankle. Honestly, her face looked more swollen than her ankle.

Quick flashback.

The second date with Google didn't go so well. Just think about it. That whole episode with Mausiji landing on the rear windshield and then the ditch. Gawd. I was in no mood to eat. (Oh, yeah, it was that bad.)

We drove around aimlessly for the first fifteen minutes. And eventually ended up at Fruit Shop on Greams Road.

'Shit, that was close,' Google groaned the minute we sat down.

Close? *Close?*

'Googs, I'm dead. Finito. Finished.'

'Shit, what're we going to do?'

'You mean, what am *I* going to do.'

'Yes, yes. What're you going to do?'

Thanks, Googs.

The waiter materialized and handed us the menu cards.

'So, what do you think?' I asked Google, a worried expression on my face.

'I'll have Jughead's Special. It's my favourite juice,' Google smiled.

'No, you dumbo! What do you think I should do? When I go back home.'

'Oh, that. Okay, how about this? Chill for now. You've been through a big shock. Give yourself some time to think, have some juice.'

I settled for a lime mint cooler. But I couldn't really enjoy it. My mind was on the emotional tsunami waiting for me at home.

To add to my woes, Google didn't happen to compliment me. On the clothes I'd so painstakingly picked. Orange skinny denims and a white frilly Benetton top. The cutesy hairband and the chunky bracelet from Accessorize also failed to draw any appreciation. Boys, bah!

Back at my place.

I ambled in and deposited my bag on the dining table.

'Mom, I'm home,' I cried out.

The two ladies practically vaulted out of their rooms.

'Why did you say Robin was picking you up?' Mom asked accusingly.

I was quiet.

'Rinki, I asked you a question,' Mom said sternly.

'Because of this, Mom,' I said in obvious frustration.

'This?' Mom raised a well-plucked eyebrow.

'All this, Mom,' I said flailing my arms about. 'This unnecessary drama, the tears, the fireworks. Gawd, I can't handle it.'

'So you're saying it's okay to lie?' Mom said, tears springing to her eyes.

'Ask her if there's something going on between her and the fat boy.' That was Mausiji, who else?

'Stay out of this, Mausiji,' Mom barked. Mom had never ever confronted me like that. Dad, yes. Mom was only too happy to hover around in the background and let Dad do all the talking. I guess, with Dad away in Coimbatore and The Mausiji Menace looming large, she'd no choice but to step into his shoes. Play Mother India, so to speak.

'Mom, please! There's nothing going on between me and Google.'

Not yet, at any rate.

'Then you should've no problem tying him this,' Mom sniffed, waving a rakhi in the air.

Oh, gawd. No idea where *that* came from! The rakhi, I mean. Raksha Bandhan was way back in August. How'd she manage to get her hands on one of those? Did Mom have a ready stock of rakhis? What else had she been hoarding all these years?

Then another terrifying thought struck me. Gosh, I didn't know my mom at all. It made me realize that *Cosmo* and all those girlie magazines were right: You could share your roof, your bed, your life with someone and not know them at all.

'No probs, Mom, no probs at all,' I said bitterly.

'So much tension,' Mausiji said dramatically. 'At this rate, I'll soon need buttocks.'

I looked at her ample posterior and wondered what on earth she was talking about. Then it struck me. She meant Botox. Of course!

I steered my thoughts to the colossal problem at hand. How on earth could I make Google my rakhi bro? I'd just started dating him, for the love of god!

Quick flashback: Back in Delhi, the whole rakhi bro thing was such a racket, I tell you. Only two kinds of girls indulged in it. The despos who badly wanted to talk to a guy without coming across as despo. And the ones out to make a quick buck.

Buying a rakhi——50 bucks.

Getting a rakhi gift——500 bucks.

Acting like a coy sister——priceless.

I buzzed Google the next day after school.

'Hi, Google,' I said without preamble. 'We need to talk.'

'So talk,' he said, blissfully unaware that he was soon going to be inducted into the Tripathi Hall of Fame.

'Not here. Meet me at CCD on KNK Road in an hour?'

'Cool. I'll pick you up.'

'No,' I said sharply, startling him. 'I'll catch a rick. Don't be late. See you soon.'

'Whatever,' Google signed off.

At CCD

'Why're you still wearing your sunglasses?'

I cast a surreptitious look around.

'I'm in trouble.'

'Why, what did you do now?' Google asked, sinking into a cushioned cane chair.

'Thanks,' I said, my tone sarci.

'Anytime, babe,' Google grinned.

I exhaled.

'Googs, my parents have asked me to . . .'

'Break off with me?'

'No, no.'

'So they approve of us?'

Us? *Us?*

'They're okay with our relationship?' Google went on excitedly.

Hang on a bloody sec. Relationship, what relationship? We'd been out on like two frickin' dates!

'Let me put it this way, Googs,' I exhaled. 'The only relationship they want us to share is that of bhaiya-behena. Get it?'

He stared at me, his mouth agape.

'Brother-sister? No way in bloody hell!'

My sentiments exactly.

I whipped the rakhi out of my bag and placed it on the table.

'You're not thinking about doing it,' Google eyed it with suspicion, fear writ large in his eyes.

'I don't know. I mean, no! Of course not. But there's crazy pressure at home. Oh god, what do I do?'

We lapsed into silence.

Google brought his right fist down on the table. *Thwaaaack!*

'Idea!'

I lifted a wary eyebrow. What now?

'Did your mausiji get a clear view of me, Rinks?'

I shrugged.

'I don't know.'

'Think, Rinks, think. If she did, we're dead. If she didn't, I've a plan.'

Well, Mausiji was short-sighted. And she hadn't been wearing her glasses during the ditch episode. Forgotten to wear them in her hurry to run down and catch me red-handed, no doubt.

'What's cooking in that head of yours, Googs?'

'Why don't we get a dummy piece? A fake rakhi brother. Like in the movies. Rinks, you can tie ten rakhis on his wrist. In full view of your family. That'll get them off your back!'

Would it? Would it? No harm trying.

'Okay, but where'd I find a dummy piece? Who'd agree to a crazy scheme like this?'

'A friend, a neighbour, a classmate,' Google threw option after option at me.

'I can't think of anyone,' I wailed.

'Well, I can,' Google drawled triumphantly, a wicked gleam in his eyes. 'You don't have the hots for Adit, do you?'

Whaaaaaat?! I didn't. Not at the moment, anyway. But he was sweet and smart and sensitive. Was I ready to write him off completely from the future? More importantly, was I ready to screw up the present? I guess not.

'Don't be silly, Google. You know I don't,' I said at last.

'Good. Then you won't have a problem asking him.'

Well, I *did* have a problem asking Adit. It's not every day you march up to a friend and ask him to become family, you know.

I mean, it was embarrassing. There was no easy way of doing it. None at all. The next day at school, all I could think of was how to break the news to Adit. God, even proposing to him would've been easier. Oh, yeah. I broke my head for two hours straight. While Bhaskar Sir explained the intricacies of trigonometry to the rest of the class, I played out the different scenarios in my mind.

Possibility 1:

Rinki (awkwardly): Adit, I wanted to ask you something.

Adit (cheerfully): Ask.

Rinki (haltingly): Will you . . . I was wondering if you . . . Could you . . .

Adit: Lend you my comic collection? Sorry, I can't do that. Ask me for anything else under the sun.

Rinki: Anything?

Adit: Anything . . .

Rinki (mustering courage): Can I tie you a rakhi?

Adit: . . . Except that.

Possibility 2:

Rinki: Adit, will you be my . . . ?

Adit (interjecting sharply): Sorry, I don't see you that way.

Rinki: Actually, I was going to say 'brother'.

Adit: Aiyyo, that's worse.

Rinki (exasperatedly): How's it worse?

Adit: If I get a rakhi tied from every girl I talk to, people will think I'm gay.

Possibility 3:

Rinki: Adit, will you be my brother?

Adit (dropping his books with a flourish): Thought you'd never ask. I've been carrying this rakhi around in my pocket ever since we met.

Bugles and conches sound. Assorted gods shower rose petals from the heavens, above like in those *Ramayana* DVDs Mom loves to watch. With a grand gesture, I proceed to tie the mighty rakhi, aka Family Friendship Band, on Adit's wrist. He beams proudly and India's Rakhi Anthem, *Phoolon ka taaron ka,* plays softly in the background.

There is someone watching after me Up There. And Down South too.

Dad got wind of the whole rakhi brother thing. It was Mom who spilled the beans. She'd expected him to take her side, no doubt, but the whole thing backfired. He was furious. Not with me. With Mom.

Dad dismissed the whole thing. Said it was ridiculous. And that tying a rakhi to a boy was no solution to the problem at hand. 'A teen has to be reasoned with, not dictated to.'

Yeah, right. I'd remind him of that the next time we had an argument.

In fact, Dad wanted to fly down in the middle of the week. Play troubleshooter, diffuse the crisis. Can you imagine? The whole bloody mess had reached *those* proportions.

Luckily, good sense prevailed. In Mom's case, that is. She decided to back off. Agreed to drop the whole rakhi business. And I was home scot-free. Yippeee!

Pity, Google didn't share my enthusiasm when I shared the good news with him.

The rakhi episode did it. Convinced me that I simply had to get Mausiji out of my way.

But how? How could Rinki Mouse possibly bell the Mausi Cat?

Out of the corner of my eye, I saw Mausiji snatching a five-hundred rupee note from Rakamma's hand.

'The radio, five hundred rupees.'

What the hell was going on?

I didn't realize I'd spoken out aloud.

'I just sold my radio to Rama,' Mausiji replied, waving the note in the air.

'You mean, Rakamma.'

'That's what I said,' Mausiji pouted.

What sort of a person sells an old piece of crap to someone poor?

'Good of me, no? Now Rama will have something to listen to,' Mausiji gloated.

That's who.

'You mean, that thing plays?' I asked innocently, gesturing, for Rakamma's sake.

Two sets of eyes bulged.

Rakamma's and Mausiji's.

'Of course it does.'

'When was the last time you played it?' I asked.

1947. I was itching to answer my question. But wisely, very wisely, I held my tongue.

Mausiji looked cross. Rakamma looked distinctly unhappy with the transaction.

'Er, um, recently only,' Mausiji attempted bravely. But the hesitation in her voice was unmistakable.

'*Venda, venda*, nahi, nahi. *Kud, kud*, give, give,' Rakamma whined, clearly changing her mind and asking for the cash.

She leapt at the note dangling from Mausiji's hand. Mausiji instantly stood on her toes and hoisted it higher. Rakamma bounded up and down. So did Mausiji. For a fraction of a second, Rakamma paused. Mausiji let her guard down. Sure enough, Rakamma made a gigantic leap and plucked the note out of Mausiji's hand.

And that gave me an idea.

'Mom, let's go for a movie,' I suggested the next day.

'Okay,' Mom agreed.

'Fine,' Mausiji nodded, jumping to her feet.

'Wait a second, I'll get my bag.' Mom made a beeline for her room.

Within minutes, we were at Sathyam theatre.

'Uh-oh,' Mom mumbled, rummaging through her Coach tote bag.

'What happened, Mom?'

'I'm out of cash.'

'No problem, Mom. I'm sure Mausiji will be happy to shell out.'

Mausiji looked anything but.

'And oh, I'm so hungry, Rinki,' Mom said, patting her stomach.

'No problem, Mom,' I said reassuringly. 'Mausiji will be more than happy to treat us to popcorn.'

'Uh, I'm out of cash too,' Mausiji said sullenly.

'No, no, Mausiji, I see a couple of notes sticking out of your bag.'

Reluctantly, she opened her bag.

'See? Right there,' I said triumphantly.

'Pity, Rakamma didn't go through with the deal. We would have been five hundred bucks richer.'

'We?' Mausiji repeated in horror.

'I'm so happy you're here, Mausiji,' I said, hugging her. After a brief moment of hesitation, Mom joined me. 'Tell her Mom. There's no shame in admitting it.'

'Admitting what?' Mausiji asked in alarm.

'Mom's credit card has been declined. Till Dad's back, you're our saviour.'

Mom sniffed.

'When's Dad back again, Mom?'

'Next weekend, I think. Not sure though.'

Mausiji waited until after the movie to declare, 'I'm really missing Delhi. Book my tickets online, Rinki.'

'Would have loved to, Mausiji. But no credit card, remember . . .'

Mausiji's expression said, 'How can I possibly forget?'

'Fine, I'll ask my son to do it.'

Chapter 10

BlackBerry Messenger Status: Bye bye Mausiji. Hello happiness.

We three, ours none. Relatives, I mean.

Mausiji was leaving. F-I-N-A-L-L-Y. The day couldn't have come sooner.

Best of all, Dad was back. His project was over and done with.

But more importantly, Mausiji was leaving.

Hurray!!! I was so looking forward to it. For more reasons than one.

You see, we've this tradition Up North. Elders give a small token of 'appreciation' to the youngsters at the time of departure. Usually hard cash. Also known as 'sagan'. Kind of a 'thank you for having me over and here's something to make up for all the trouble I caused'. Something good was going to come out of Mausiji's visit, after all.

I'd already decided what I was going to do with the money. Say she'd give me around one grand. (500–1000 bucks were the norm. With another hundred bucks thrown in, to make it an auspicious amount). There was this cute shimmery top I'd been eyeing at Esprit. It'd look great with my narrow-leg Levi's jeans. The minute Mausiji was out of the house, I'd go flying to Express Avenue Mall to buy it. Oh, yeah.

I woke up early to bid her a teary farewell. Mom and Dad bent down and touched her feet. At least they pretended to. Usually, people just make a big show of bending down. So if they reach halfway down, it's a big thing. Mom and Dad had reached her knees when Mausiji suddenly spoke up.

'Oh, I forgot,' she exclaimed.

Here it comes, I thought. My excitement levels were about to go through the roof.

'Do you have a couple of hundred-rupee notes? It'd be good to have change at the airport. Never know when you need to buy something.'

Gosh, I was so flabbergasted. She was asking *us* for sagan. The cheek!

Obediently, Dad fished out a couple of hundreds. Mausiji coolly pocketed them. She didn't even bless me properly, you know. She was in such a tearing hurry to reach the main door of the house. I'm just glad she didn't knock me down.

The door shut with a decisive click. I slumped on the sofa, feeling like an Olympic weightlifter who'd just finished lifting three hundred kilograms.

Rinki Tripathi is taking an online quiz on Teenz Forever.

Online Quiz # 566. Styloo or stinkoo: What are you?

1. You see the latest issue of *Vogue* lying on your coffee table. You:

a. Tear a page and wrap your sandwiches in it

b. Pounce on it like a hungry dog would on a bone

2. According to you, Armani is:

   a. Your Sindhi friend's cousin

   b. Your style guru

3. High heels or keds, your choice would be:

   a. Hawai chappals

   b. Stilettos

4. The last time you applied make-up was:

   a. During your VI grade Halloween party

   b. I never take it off

5. To up your style quotient, you'd:

   a. Watch Lok Sabha TV

   b. Read fashion mags, surfing the net, befriending stylish folk

If you scored mostly As: Please do us a favour. Sign out. Now. Please. There's no point, really. We shouldn't even be corrupting you with evil thoughts like fashion, style, being human. We hope you're happy wherever you reside. Under a rock, in a cave, beehive, whatever. We just pray we never run into you. Ever.

If you scored mostly Bs: Quite the style goddess, aren't you? You have got your fashion fundas right. And boy, are we waiting to hear from you! In fact, right this moment, we're looking for freelancers for our weekly fashion column. So, what you waiting for? Send us a brief (and we mean brief) note about yourself, with a short sample of your writing skills and we'll get back to you ASAP.

Rinki Tripathi scored only Bs.

Chapter 11

BlackBerry Messenger Status: Caught and bowled!

It was that time of the year again. When the little moth in me turned into a butterfly. Time for School Culturals.

I sighed in relief.

'Thank god, life without Culturals is like hair without hair colour. Dull, boring, black,' I told Robin.

'Wow, Rinks, you sound like the brand ambassador of L'Oreal.'

I took a bow.

'So, what's it going to be this year?' Robin wanted to know.

'I don't know. I'm hoping to be made fashion show co-ordinator,' I said with a modest shrug.

Quick flashback. I'd suggested the theme and costumes for last year's inter-school fashion show. It had gone on to become a huge hit. The rest, as they say, was history, geography, math. It was, as Barney Stinson of *How I Met Your Mother* fame would say, legen—wait for it—dary! In fact, I was lock-kiya-jaaye sure that the Cultural Secretary, Manju, would march up to me anytime and ask me to do the honours. But days passed and I didn't hear from her.

'Rinks, the problem with you is that you think too much,' Google said when I confided in him later that week.

We were at the Backyard. Robin had made a guest appearance that day.

'I agree,' she said, raising her glass of Sprite on the rocks.

'Why don't you take a chill pill, machan? I mean, the show is still two weeks away. I'm sure she will call you any day now.'

'But there is no time. There's stuff to be planned, costumes to be stitched . . .'

'Shouldn't the fashion show coordinator be worried about that?'

'But I'm the fashion show coordinator!'

'Correction,' Google interrupted. 'You're hoping to be appointed fashion show coordinator.'

Talk about stating the obvious.

'Until that happens, why don't you just enjoy your drink?'

'Cheers,' I said gloomily.

Turned out I was right. The very next week, a li'l bird told Robin that Manju had chosen Krithika to be the fashion show coordinator. Krithika! I mean, the whole thing was such a joke. Krithika wouldn't know fashion if it hit her on the head. She was such a fuddy-duddy. The unfairness of it all made me want to weep.

'Robin, do I go and confront her?' I asked, clenching my fists and teeth.

'Who, Krithika?'

'No, Manju. I'd like to know what's going on in that head of hers. Does she want CBVB to win or not?'

'Rinks, calm down. Take a deep breath.'

'No, Robin. I'm not going to calm down. How dare she do this to me? How dare she?' I thundered.

I jumped to my feet. 'I'm going to get to the bottom of this,' I said, brushing past Robin.

'Rinki, wait!'

But I was in no mood to listen.

I crossed over the courtyard, ran past the lunching students and went straight to XII A. Manju was sitting all by herself. She was digging into her lunch box *and* poring over a textbook, all at once. Lovely, I thought to myself. And such people were going to decide the fashion future of the school.

I cleared my throat. She looked up, startled. I crossed my arms over my chest (in what I hoped to be an adequately aggressive gesture) and glared down at her.

'Oh, it's you, Rinki.'

'Oh, so you do know who I am.'

Her eyes blinked rapidly behind her thick glasses.

'What? Of course, I know who you are. Who doesn't?'

I narrowed my eyes. What the hell was that supposed to mean?

'Don't act cute,' I snapped.

'What?' she parroted again.

'I don't know what kind of a game you're playing, Manju. But I don't like it. I don't like it at all.'

'Hey, hang on, Rinki. What are you talking about?'

'You don't know what I'm talking about?' I challenged.

She shook her head.

God, either she was acting dumb or she was one dumb chica.

'May I ask why I haven't been chosen to be fashion coordinator?'

'Oh, that.'

'Yes, *that*. It may be a small thing for you, busy as you are with your books,' I added cattily. 'But it happens to be very important to me.'

'Didn't Mrs Verghese tell you?'

'Mrs Verghese! Where did she come into the picture?'

Manju got to her feet and squeezed my shoulder gently.

'She's the picture and the photo frame and the wall, my dear.'

'She asked you not to pick me for the post?' I asked her, my voice small.

Just seconds ago, I'd felt like a pretty balloon. Poised to go up, up, up in the blue sky. As the seconds ticked by, the air just went out of me.

'In our Princy's words, "academically weak students don't get to be on organizing committees".'

I gasped.

What did marks have to do with it? Some of us were good at academics, others took the sports arena by storm and then there were the cultural queen bees, like yours truly. It was like expecting our Prime Minister to open the Indian innings at the T-20 World Cup. It was like anticipating Katrina to win the Spell Bee Contest. It was like waiting for Sachin to paint the Mona Lisa.

I mean, why the hell was our Princy mixing up the issues?

Manju shrugged. 'I've no idea, Rinki. If you don't believe me, you could go ask her.'

Like hell I was going to ask her.

I could only just imagine the conversation. Shudder!

'I see. So she decided to make Miss Fuddy-duddy the coordinator,' I fumed.

Manju shrugged for what must've been the hundredth time.

'This is so unfair. That post should've been mine. Mine, mine, mine.'

I turned on my heel to storm out of the class and nearly bumped into the unfairly crowned Queen of Fashion, Krithika.

No problem there. Except she also happened to be Mrs Verghese's pet, mugpot, cry baby, bad sport and sore loser, all rolled into one. But I didn't know that then.

The next thing I knew I was standing in Mrs Verghese's office, a blotchy-faced Kry, er, Krithika next to me.

I was quaking in my boots. Robin was right. Google was right. I did think too much. Wayyy too much. It was my overthinking that did me in. All the $%#@ time.

Look where it landed me. In the lion's (or lioness's, in this case. Oh, hell, do we have to be politically correct at a time like this!) den, no less. The lioness was waiting to pounce on me. But not before it stalked the prey for good measure.

Mrs Verghese took off her glasses and placed them on the table.

Uh-oh, bad news. This meant she was in a foul, foul mood. Robin had tremendous body language skills and last year, she'd taken great pains to teach me and Sudha what Princy's gestures meant.

'Rinki Tripathi, perhaps you'll care to explain what this mess is all about?'

My voice got lost in my throat.

'W-w-what mess, Ma'am?' I squeaked.

'I hear you've been accusing Krithika of stealing your rightful position.'

I wanted to shoot *Kry*thika a look of pure hatred. But I thought the better of it. It was so not going to help my case.

'Er, I don't remember saying that, Ma'am.'

'Oh! Then let me refresh your memory. I think what you said was: "It was my position. Mine, mine, mine."'

Did she really have to repeat that? Word for word?

Krithika's sobs were jamming to an invisible orchestra. They grew louder every time her name was mentioned. But when faults were being found with me, they were barely a muffled whisper.

'Is it true, Rinki?' Mrs Verghese propped her arms on the table and leaned forward. As if she could pierce through my skin and read my mind.

'Um, I must've said words to that effect.'

'The question is, why did you say those hurtful words?'

I studied my shoes. Krithika's sobs had reached boiling point. I thought the glass window would shatter any time.

Mrs Verghese leaned back in her swivelling chair. 'I wonder what gives you that sense of entitlement. Do you really think you can bully your way into everything?'

I nearly sputtered. Me? Bully? I was anything but. Anyone who knew me could vouch for that.

'Anyway, it is not for you to decide. It is my decision. Mine, mine, mine.'

Ouch!

'You may leave now. Just stop acting all high and mighty, Miss Tripathi.' She gave me a look that could melt all the polar ice caps in the world. Case dismissed.

'Sir, yes, sir,' I nearly barked and clicked my heels like the cadets do in all those war movies.

From Chennai Super Chick's Blog

People,

> *There's good news and bad news.*

> *Bad news: I'm not going to be the fashion show coordinator at the culturals. Sob, sob.*

> *Good news: I'm so over it.*

> *As my friend R likes to say, 'It doesn't matter!'*

> *It so doesn't. I mean, I have better things to do with my time.*

> *Teach you make-up tricks, for instance.*

> *Hmm, so here are two cool looks coming up. Just for you, my beauties:*

> ### Day Look—Fresh, dewy, angelic

> *For this look, just dab on a good moisturizer all over your face.*

> *Not too much, or your face will look oily. Not too little, or it'll look dry.*

> *Go with your skin type and choose a heavy or light formula.*

> *Add a hint of peach blush. It's good for all skin types. Fairer skin tones, have fun with pinks.*

> *Line your eyes with kohl. Don't rub it in till your skin peels off. Just a thin line will do.*

Compete your look with a neutral shade of gloss.

As for the hair, just leave it loose. Nothing too elaborate. And you're all set to face the day. Lunch date, movie, day at a pal's, bingo!

Night Look—smoky, mysterious, diva-ish

Trade the moisturizer for a foundation.

Coat your eyes with mascara. Use eyeliner. Wing it at the corner of the eyes. Dark lips.

Now for hair. If you've a curly mop, straighten it, and vice versa. Nice to try out something different.

Happy night out in town, gurlzzzz!

Lau,

Chennai Super Chick

Chapter 12

BlackBerry Messenger Status: The coolest cold shoulder in the world . . .

Teachers have different ways of punishing you. You know that, of course. Some throw dusters at you, some throw *you* out of the classroom (making you an 'out-standing' student), some make you stand on chairs. But our accounts teacher, Madhavan Sir, had a unique way of expressing his anger: He'd simply refuse to look at the students while taking lessons.

It was the stuff legends are made of. The story of Maddy Sir's infamous tantrums had been passed down to every newbie at CBVB. Just imagine. One whole hour of a teacher teaching while staring at the walls or outside the window. I only hoped that when it happened I wouldn't be sitting in the first row.

One fine day, I finally had my wish. In the name of teaching us, Maddy Sir was reading the textbook. Out loud. When *Clang!* A pencil box fell to the floor.

Maddy Sir paused. He pushed his glasses down his nose and glared at us.

Silence.

He went back to his reading.

Clang!

Maddy Sir continued to read as if nothing had happened.

Four more pencil boxes fell in quick succession.

Clang! Clang! Clang! Clang!

Maddy Sir snapped the textbook shut with a frightening bang.

'One more clang and just you see!' Maddy Sir said in his most threatening voice.

Sudha was so nervous at the declaration that her fingers slipped and *Clang!*

'You people, very worst,' he lamented, before taking the *Bhishmapratigya* (epic swear), 'I shall not look you guys in the eye for the rest of the year.' The bookworms of the class, led by Balachandran, begged and pleaded with him. But their chamchagiri fell on deaf ears.

Maddy Sir's mood was off. And the fun was on.

For the next few days, Class XII C was on a roll. So was I. Ahem! I decided to make the most of Maddy Sir's Sulking Sessions. So I carried an armload of books, comics and magazines to school every day.

I managed to revisit my entire collection of *Princess Diaries*. No kidding. Robin finished reading *Breaking Dawn*.

Sudha finished doodling a lovely sketch of Google. For me, of course. I'd finally broken the news to the girls. About me dating Google. To her credit, Sudha had been extremely understanding about the whole thing. Thank god.

Robin, on the other hand, thought I was crazy to go on dates in XII grade. Just because her boyfriend was away in Manipal and she couldn't. Silly goose. But she'd no problem with my choice of date per se. Thanks again, god.

Anyway, right across from us, even Mr Goody Two-shoes Balachandran gave in to temptation. He polished off *podi* idlis (super soft idlis garnished with red chilly powder in ghee—yummy!). The entire last row played 'Killer Killer' religiously. You know, the game where you pick lots and the one who picks the 'Killer' chit 'kills' someone by winking at them, and the rest of the group has to guess his identity.

Well, Maddy Sir hadn't counted on our indifference. Thinking it was the crucial year, he'd expected the class to be slightly more repentant.

No such luck. On the contrary, most of us wanted to kiss the kind souls who'd dropped their pencil boxes. How else could we have sampled this seasonal delight?

The thing was, a huge majority of the students were taking tuitions. They couldn't care less whether Maddy Sir finished the portions or not. The rest of the class knew it was only a matter of time before Maddy Sir went back on his word.

When I BBM-ed Ankita and told her all about the incident, she was so 'j'. She wanted her very own Maddy Sir. And she wanted him to teach not just accounts but every subject under the sun. Guess everyone can't be that lucky ☹.

Too bad, we ran out of luck pretty soon. As the saying goes, all good things must come to an end. Early the next week, Maddy Sir was back to doing what he did second best. Reading out the syllabus aloud.

And that brought out the Bunking Beast in me.

What better way to cut classes than to be part of the Culturals? Though I'd been booted out of the head honcho's job, I could certainly apply for the flunkey's post.

I went up to Krithika.

'Hi, Kry, er, Krithiks!' I chirped.

'Hi,' she said, stone-faced.

'Um, I was feeling terrible at the way things turned out . . .'

'Yes, Mrs Verghese was so mean to you,' Krithika said promptly.

'Don't worry about that,' I said with an embarrassed laugh.

'I won't,' Krithika said resolutely.

Shoot.

The straightforward approach was so not going to work. And if she thought I was going to grovel, she couldn't be more . . . right. Hey, it was the fashion show committee. Would you miss the premier show of a movie, just because you didn't get balcony tickets? Same logic.

Krithika started walking away.

'Hey, Kry, er, Krithiks, your hair looks so good. What's your secret?' I asked, hot on her heels.

'Don't know. I haven't washed it in a week.'

I was sorry I asked.

'It gets too greasy too soon.'

One week was too soon?

'You could try talcum powder,' I said kindly.

'Good tip. I suppose you could come give me a hand.'

Thought you'd never ask.

I joined her at the auditorium. Eight sleepy somethings (male and female) were waiting. Oh god, all of them looked as if they were miles away. From fashion.

'How do we go about this?' asked one bored soul.

Krithika had no freaking clue. She stood frozen in her spot. I'd no choice but to take over.

'We'll begin with the theme. Let's do something different. It's our final year, after all. Let's give them something to talk about. Any ideas, Krithika?'

She opened her mouth and shut it just as quickly.

Guessed as much.

'Okay then. How about Angels and Demons?'

Some life seemed to seep into the group.

'Sounds good,' one of the sleepy somethings murmured.

'Let's divide the team into Angels and Demons. Krithika?'

'But how do I know who'll make a good Angel and who'll make a great Devil?' she pouted.

'It's Demons. Never mind, I'll pick them. You three step aside. You'll be Angels. The rest of you . . .'

'Demons,' they chorused.

'Each Angel will be dressed in . . .'

'White,' Krithika finished enthusiastically.

'Correct answer. You've become a crorepati.'

'What?'

'Nothing,' I said quickly. 'Their props will be . . . Krithika, are you taking notes . . . wand, halo, wings. Demons, you'll be dressed in red and black. Your props? Whip, tails and horns. Am I clear?'

Krithika nodded.

'Right. Let's move on to the music . . .'

It was hard work, but it paid off. I don't mean to boast or anything. But days later, the fashion show surpassed last year's. And that's saying something. In fact, at the end, Mrs Verghese came backstage.

'I knew I'd made the right choice,' she gushed, patting Krithika on the back.

Krithika burst into tears. 'But, Ma'am, I didn't do anything. It was Rinki.'

'Rinki all the way,' the team said in unison.

The Princy looked gobsmacked.

'Well, I'm glad the show wasn't an unmitigated disaster,' she said, recovering fast.

And that was, by far, the biggest compliment she ever paid me.

I was going to watch a Tamil movie. On the big screen. Yay!

Hang on, it was not my idea. It was Robin's. She was a big fan, cooler, AC (PJ alert!) of Superstar Rajinikanth. Well, one of his biggest hits had just been re-released, and Robin was dying to catch it.

There was just one hitch. The movie was running in a kind of seedy theatre. It wasn't safe for us girls to go traipsing there. And waiting for the CD was out of the question. Tamil movie piracy had been wiped out (as good as) from the state a couple of years back. Which only meant one thing. A cajoling session with the boys.

Adit, at least, had a genuine reason. He was going to Tirupathi to seek divine blessings for the Board Exams. He couldn't very well cancel that just so that we could seek out our god of the big screen. Which left us with only one choice.

'Rinki, please ask Google,' Robin pleaded.

'No way. He'll kill me.'

'It might be the last movie I watch this year. At least give it a shot.'

So I did.

Google refused outright.

'Chance *illa*. I cannot waste three hours of my life at a theatre.'

'Says the guy who plays video games all day on Saturday,' I said archly.

'It's Saturday. I'm allowed to do what I want on weekends. What, you want to take away my freedom now?' he asked dramatically.

'Google, please, we're begging you.'

'No way, machan.'

'Okay, how about this . . . If you come along, I'll treat you at Tuscana.'

Quick clarification: Tuscana Pizzeria served these awesome thin crust pizzas. It helped that Google was as nuts about it as Robin was about Rajini.

'Now you girls are talking,' he conceded. 'Where's the movie playing?'

'Devima Theatre.'

'God, *I* may get molested there,' Googled groaned.

'Don't be such a wuss. Tell you what, I'll treat you right after the movie.'

Yes, I was willing to treat Hungry Wolf Googs at Tuscana. I wanted to see the movie that badly, but not because of Rajini. It was the First Day, First Show factor. You see, Down South, fan clubs of superstars perform these cool rituals right before they play the movie: *Abhishekam* (pouring milk) on the hero's cut-out), garlanding it, and showering petals and coins on the screen as the credits rolled.

I'd heard loads about it from Robin and Sudha. Boy, was I dying to experience it first-hand!

Bunking was a big risk but I was willing to take it. A small cost to pay for big cine dreams.

We had everything planned to the T. We'd leave home in the morning—in our school uniforms and all. But instead of going to the bus stop, we'd walk a little ahead. Where our getaway car with Google at the wheel would be waiting. Google, poor thing, had to do this three times. In three different areas of the city.

I was the last one he picked up, because I stayed closest to the theatre. Basically, I had to hide behind a tree down the road. For a good one hour too. And pray Mom wouldn't suddenly step out.

When Googs and Gang finally drove up, I jumped into the back.

Google's coolers (sunglasses) were perched on the back of his tee. Tightest of the tight tees. Here was our Southern Sallu in the making.

'Drive us to Harrisons Hotel,' I hissed. The hotel was down the road. We made a pit stop there, to get out of our uniforms.

Google parked the car.

'Girls, follow my lead. Walk in with full attitude.

'Let no one suspect that you're here just to use the bathroom,' Google continued. 'Trust me, I've done this millions of times.'

He pushed his chest out and walked towards the guard.

Fifteen minutes later, three girls in jeans and matching tees walked out. The guard's eyebrows shot up at the unexpected sight. Much like Dad's did when he saw Mom's shopping bills.

Quick confession: The theatre was kind of dingy. And the crowd was kind of scary.

It was crazy in the stands. Thank god, we were cocooned in the balcony.

Sadly, each time Rajini delivered a heavy-duty dialogue, it was Google who wolf-whistled and clapped the loudest. Much to the annoyance of our fellow movie buffs.

'*Thambi*, silence maintain, pliz,' the guys next to him, behind him, in front of him, snarled repeatedly. (*Thambi*, as in, young brother.)

'Sorry, unkils,' Google said unrepentantly. (Unkils was Google speak for 'uncles'.)

But when the next fight sequence happened, Google forgot all his good intentions and burst into spontaneous applause. And whistled non-stop for the next one minute.

'Yo, *thambi*, control,' the burly man next to him threatened.

That was it. Google lost it big time and got to his feet.

'Otherwise?' he challenged.

Burly man got to his feet too and cocked a thumb at him. This went on for five minutes.

'*Enna*?' Google asked menacingly.

'*Enna*?' burly man countered.

Enna, by the way, means 'what' in Tamil.

Time to point out the differences between Chennai and Delhi yet again. In Chennai, people will cock their thumbs at each other and argue till kingdom come. In the same amount of time, Delhiites, however, will plant a few well-aimed punches and be done with it.

Right before the interval, Google's three 'unkils' had had enough of his rowdy ways. They converged on him, and threatened to haul him out of the theatre.

'Rinki, let's go,' Robin urged.

My eyes were glued to the screen. Rajini had only just begun beating the crap out of the villains.

I'd half a mind to leave Google to his fate, but Robin gave me a hard shove. I grudgingly followed her and Sudha out of the auditorium.

'So much for bringing our personal security officer,' I cribbed outside.

Google grimaced. 'If you girls hadn't been around, I would've given them good.'

Yeah, right.

'Where to?' he asked us as we clambered into his car.

We scratched our heads. We couldn't go to Tuscana just yet. It was still 11.30. Some time before lunch.

Bessie (Besant Nagar Beach) would've been a great idea. But being out on a blazing Chennai afternoon is like going up to goons and asking them to hit you.

'How about Spencer Plaza?' Robin suggested.

Spencer Plaza was the official refuge for the jobless folk of Chennai. Why? It was a mall, it was air conditioned and it had a food court. In other words, something for everyone.

And that's where we found ourselves for the rest of the morning. We did what all jobless souls do. Went into the stores, oohed and aahed over the display. But just when the shopkeepers got all excited, we pretended to check the price tag, shook our heads and walked out, leaving them totally crushed.

We did this for two hours straight. Right till our stomachs grumbled. Then it was on to Tuscana. Gosh, we hogged like there was no tomorrow. As if someone was putting us on the next plane to Somalia. Garlic bread, Greek salad, pasta, pizza, tiramisu, panna cotta—we ordered and ate everything.

Each time a dish was cleared, we asked the steward, 'What else do you have?' I was kind of worried that in the end the manager'd come out and day, 'Sprinkle salt all over and eat me. There's nothing left.'

I don't know whether it was the cheap thrill of bunking school or what, but we had a whale of a time. In fact, I couldn't wait to bunk school again.

Too bad, I was in XII grade. Like my parents and teachers said, it was time to sober down and start taking life seriously. But as Google reminded me, that's what old age was for.

From Chennai Super Chick's Blog
I'd like to dedicate this post to certain losers.*

Move over Chamak Challo, *step aside* Munna, *run along* Munni, Kolaveri Di *is here!*

Ohmyyygosh! What a track! What a voice! What an idea, Sirji! I loooooooooooooooooooove Kolaveri Di.

I love what Kolaveri *has done for music, for Chennai, for me. My life colour . . . uuu . . . white . . . uuu . . . my future . . . . .uuu . . . bright . . . uuu . . .*

Kolaveri Di *has gone viral, my FB wall's filled with posts from all my loser pals from Delhi, and suddenly, I'm cool.*

They want to know what it means (murderous rage). They want to download it. They want it for their ring tone. I mean, they just can't get enough of Kolaveri.

And the singer, Dhanush.

It makes me want to ask all those snotty people north of the Vindhyas, 'What's up, guys? No more Rajini jokes, huh?'

Acting like big pistas only to have their noses rubbed in the ground. Ha! Serves them right for looking their Northie noses down on us.

Let's see some Bollywood actor match this.

My only problem with Kolaveri? Why, oh why, didn't it release earlier? To be precise, a year back when I moved to Chennai. I would've been spared all those barbs by my catty pals Up North.

Anyway. So what if the timing could've been better? The song was purrfect just the way it was. Thank you, Di.

*No names. They know who they are.

Chapter 13

BlackBerry Messenger Status: My very own SRK and Sallu.

Remember how I envied Bella because she had both Edward and Jacob vying for her attention? Well, I didn't any more. Take it from me, it is so not cool having two guys in your life. At the same time, that is.

Ask moi.

I had two and I wanted to tear my hair out. Not that I was doing a Bella and seeing one (Edward) and leading another on (Jacob). But still. All the snapping, the bitchy comments, the taunts. And they say girls are bitchy. After a while, I just couldn't handle it. The dudes were acting like India–Pak, Congress–BJP, SRK and Sallu.

I don't know why or how the whole rivalry started. I'd barely finished introducing them and Bam! They took an instant dislike to each other. Sigh. Why did life have to be so complicated? I had better things to be worried about, you know. Pre-Boards, Mrs Verghese, tuitions, my parents. But there I was, biting my nails over the next Adit–Google confrontation.

It was time to play peacemaker. I just had to bring them together. Make them see that they had a lot in common (besides me).

So I did the best thing under the circumstances. Drew up a list.

Things Google and Adit have in common:

1. Good listeners
2. Friendly
3. Helpful
4. Caring

Things they don't:

1. Adit was hard-working, Google was hardly working
2. Adit weighed his decisions, Google's motto was 'act first, think later or not at all'
3. If something was not working out, Adit would let go. But somehow or the other, Google would find some jugaad, a way to work around the problem
4. Adit loved learning new things, Google believed he knew everything worth knowing

Time was running out. Pre-Boards were hovering around the corner and I needed them both. Adit, because he appealed to my sane side. Google, because he fed my crazy self. I was feeling so torn lately, courtesy, their polar opposite views on every subject.

Example:

The Google Approach

Rinki: Google, I know someone who is setting the Maths paper.

Google: That's fantastic! Let's buy the paper right away. How much do we have to pay him?

The Adit Approach

Rinki: Adit, I know someone who is setting the Maths paper.

Adit: That's fantastic. Work hard, score well and impress the guy. Imagine how happy he's going to be when you score centum.

Of course, this is not a hypothetical example. It really happened. It was Google who sprang it on me.

We were at the Backyard one Friday evening. I was swigging beer (one can of Corona Light, supplied by Google's personal bootlegger Neha). I so didn't want to overdo it. There were many suspicious types at home, just waiting to 'sniff' things out.

Google took a sip, leaned back on the bolster and looked me straight in the eye.

'Rinks, how much dough do you have?'

'About five hundred bucks,' I replied.

'Not in your pocket, dummy! I mean, how much do you have in all? At home, in your piggy bank, under your pillow?'

Umm, that.

'Why do you want to know?' I began cautiously.

'Because there is an opportunity of a lifetime waiting. And like all good opportunities, it costs money.'

I didn't know good opportunities cost money. In Googleland, maybe. But in the real world, opportunities came free. Or so I thought.

'You and your hare-brained ideas,' I said dismissively.

'Remember, Rinks, there is no such thing as a free lunch,' Google said wisely. 'All we need is ten grand. Ten grand and we are all set.'

'Set? For what?'

'For the Pre-board Business Math paper.'

My jaw dropped. 'You're kidding,' I protested.

He had to be. No way. He couldn't pull off something like that. Sure, buying question papers wasn't unheard of. People had been buying them for generations now. Just that I never thought *I* could be one of those someday.

Hmm. I guess if anyone could pull it off, it was Google.

'Pakka, promise, swear,' Google said solemnly.

'You mean, you can get us the question paper?'

He nodded. 'Sure can.'

'But how?'

'Show a little faith, girl. Take my word for it.'

'B-b-but . . .' I blubbered.

'Have I ever let you down?'

'No.'

'Have I ever made a promise I can't keep?'

'Nope.'

'Have I ever made tall claims?'

'Not at all.'

'So, if I say I can get the paper, I can get the paper.'

'But . . .'

'No ifs and buts. Are you in or out?'

I chewed on my lower lip. It was tempting. Getting the question paper would solve a lot of my problems. Hell, it'd solve all my problems! My parents would get off my back. Mrs

Verghese would leave me alone. I could spend time on things I really loved doing. Write my blog, read fashion magazines, spend more time online, hang out with friends, watch movies, listen to music, etc. etc.

But still. There were the risks to think of. And they were huge. What if someone found out? The humiliation, the punishments! I got the chills just thinking about them. Plus, what if it was all bull? As in, it was all a big scam? They didn't have the right paper and were looking for innocent students to fleece? Gawd, I'd not only be a couple of grand poorer, but would also have to repeat a year.

Google held up a hand.

'I know what you're thinking. As usual, you are over thinking.'

I stayed mum.

'Admit it, Rinks. You're thinking of every possible thing that could go wrong.'

I shrugged.

'Okay, how about this . . . What if we study and buy the paper?'

Well, that sounded reasonable. Kind of. I considered his proposal. I could hear the minutes tick in Google's brain.

'Hmm, I guess you've a point. That way we could have the best of both worlds.'

'Now we're talking,' Google exulted. 'Okay, so how much can you pool in?'

'Two grand, maybe three?' I'd stashed some money aside. For a good cause. And what could be better than the pursuit of education?

'Okay, we need more people to contribute to the Scheme.'

'Scheme?' I repeated, raising an eyebrow.

'Exam Relief and Student Welfare Scheme.'

'I could ask Robin and Sudha and . . .' I hesitated.

'Go on, ask that wuss Adit, I have no objections. But ask them all to zip their lips. Don't want word to get out.'

Oh my god, it was all so, so stressful! But I had to try.

Tackling Robin and Sudha proved far easier than I'd expected. Robin was no longer the old Robin. The ant, the hard worker. She was a girl in love. And like all girls in love, she spent most of her time on the phone. Being in a long-distance relationship didn't help. In a nutshell, she needed help and she needed it bad. She agreed to pool in a grand.

Google took on the task of convincing Sudha. She barely needed convincing. Hey, Google could've asked her for her kidneys and she'd only be happy to comply. That was another one grand.

Final Finances for Business Math Paper Stood at:
Rinki—3k

Google—3k

Robin—1k

Sudha—1k

Grand Total—8k
We needed two thousand more. In other words, we needed Adit. But who'd bell the cat? Robin? Sudha?

The unanimous decision was, who else but poor ole me.

Let me tell you something. I've had to do many tough things in my life. Move cities, change schools, leave my best friend behind, face criticism (and not just for my weight), live with difficult parents (and one troublesome grandaunt), go through a devastating heartbreak (a certain Mr TJ) and so on. But convincing Adit to come on board proved to be the biggest challenge. By far.

I completely lost my nerve. That was in the beginning.

And by the time I got around to approach him, I lost my hearing as well.

'WHAT THE HELL DO YOU MEAN? Are you out of your mind, Rinki Tripathi? Do you know what you're saying? What are you doing with your life? Are you a criminal? Is that why you want to commit this crime? You're buying a question paper today, you will want to murder someone next? Let me tell you, Rinki Tripathi, I'll have no part of it. In fact, I will go one step forward and say I'LL NOT LET YOU DO IT.'

'Adit, just listen to me,' I pleaded.

'No, Rinki Tripathi, you listen to me. I've had enough of you and your stupid ideas. You've been up to no good since the time I met you. But this, this is too much. Even for you. I've had enough. Please leave me alone. And take it from me, you are asking for trouble. Mend your ways now! Before it is too late. OR YOU WILL LIVE TO REGRET IT.'

WTF?! I mean, he sounded like my parents. Crime, murder, regret. What crap! And why on earth was he addressing me by my full name? What on earth was *that* about? For god's sake. He was acting totally unhinged. So he didn't want to buy the paper. Hey, he could've just said so. Easy peasy.

Yeah. It certainly wasn't me who'd lost it. It was him. What else could explain the outburst? It wasn't normal to get worked up over something so trivial. He could've just said 'no'.

A firm, simple NO. That's all. Instead, he got totally worked up and looked as if he'd have a heart attack.

I mean, what was with all the name calling and finger pointing? I didn't ask him to be friends with me. He wasn't doing me a favour. And honestly, if he had such a superiority complex, we were better off not being friends.

Such thoughts were running in my mind. Guess I was totally unprepared for what came next. Really. He rushed inside his room. I thought he'd lose some steam and eventually come out. But you know what? He came running back with a stack of religious books.

'Rinki Tripathi, put your hand on these books and swear that you'll do no such thing.'

I was speechless. God, he was one crazy dude. Did he really think I'd give up on the whole idea (and in the process, on my dreams)? Just because he subjected me to a moral lecture?

What was this, some melodramatic movie? Where the villain sees the error of his ways and repents after a tongue-lashing by the hero? Gawd.

I finally found my voice.

'I shall do no such thing,' I said.

Adit let out a sigh of relief.

'Swear on a stack of holy books, that is,' I said, sounding way calmer than I felt.

Adit's eyes bulged and his face turned a peculiar shade of red. For a minute, I thought he was going to strangle me then and there.

The silence was deafening. Then out of the blue, my stomach grumbled loudly. It was past four in the evening and I hadn't had a morsel to eat since morning.

Adit flung the books aside and stormed out of the room. It must've been THE wildest thing he'd ever done in his life.

'So you didn't get two grand from Adit,' Google said, giving me a pitying look.

I was sooo annoyed. I mean, was the guy even listening? I'd just told him the entire sorry story and that's all he had to say?

'Google, I don't think you get it.'

'Oh, I do get it. You were just too chicken to ask your boy wonder for some money.'

That got my goat.

'For one, Adit is not my boy wonder. In fact, I wonder if he's human. Second of all, there was no question of asking him for money. Not after the way he insulted me.'

'But he didn't say anything offensive.'

I sprang to my feet.

'You may be used to such insults from friends, Google. But it was a first for me.'

Google opened his mouth to speak but in the end, he held his tongue. Wisely so. I was in no mood to stomach another jibe. I swung my school bag over my shoulder and walked out, slamming the door behind me for good measure.

But in the end, I didn't. Buy the paper, after all. Oh, it wasn't because of Adit. It wasn't because of that YouTube clipping of Anna Hazare that Adit forwarded me. It wasn't even because we couldn't raise the funds to purchase the damn thing.

It was something else. Something totally unexpected.

Robin and I had gone to Google's one evening. To seal the deal.

We found Google's left ear glued to the cell. And he was screaming bloody murder.

It was like some scene from a stock exchange movie. Only thing, instead of the economy, something wayyyy bigger was at stake. Our lives.

'You double crosser! You $%^#! I will kill you! This is my life, we are talking about here. MY LIFE. It's not a joke, you #$%%% piece of @#$.'

At one point, Robin actually stuffed her fingers into her ears.

I, on the other hand, leaned forward. He was using some really colourful abuses. Ones I'd never heard before. And it was all I could do to stop myself from jotting them down in my diary.

He hung up after what seemed like an eternity.

We waited patiently.

'What was all that about, Google?'

'&*^%! Rinki, Robin, we are screwed!'

'What???'

'Turns out the guy *was* selling fake papers to everyone, that basket!'

Robin and I exchanged a glance.

'Thank god we didn't end up buying the paper,' Robin said at last.

Google threw his cell aside in a fit of disgust.

'Thank god? Thank god for what? For the cheat who ran away with our money?'

My blood ran cold. No! Google wouldn't have been such an idiot. I mean, who makes an advance payment to a crook?

'No need to panic, guys,' Robin said, at last, looking unnaturally calm. But I knew she was all shaken up. She had to be. We were XII graders, for god's sake. We had no finances. Debt, yes. Lots of it. But money, zilch. And everything we had, we'd given Google. For the paper man who was supposed to sell us the question paper. Bloody hell!

'Surely you didn't pay him an advance?' Robin asked hopefully. The quiver in her voice was unmistakable.

'No.'

Robin and I almost wept in relief.

'I paid him the full amount.'

There was pin-drop silence in the room. And then I exploded. Spewing the very same abuses Google had been showering on the paper man seconds ago.

Rinki Tripathi is taking an online quiz on Teenz Forever.

Quiz # 828. Straight arrow or wild child: what are you?

1. Your parents give you one grand for textbooks. They cost Rs. 600. You:
   a. Blow the remaining 400 bucks on yourself (it's your money, after all)
   b. Dutifully return the balance
2. You borrow your friend's top. It ends up with a small tear. You:
   a. Return it like nothing happened
   b. Come clean with her and offer to buy her a new top

3. You find a hundred-rupee note lying on the campus. You:
   a. Coolly pocket the cash (finders keepers, losers weepers)
   b. Hand it to your class teacher
4. Your friend is blamed for something you've done. You:
   a. Let her take the rap (it's what friends are for)
   b. 'Fess up (it's the right thing to do)
5. Your friend's super-hot BF asks you out on a date. You:
   a. Ask 'what're you doing this Saturday?'
   b. Report it to your friend

If you've scored mostly As: Babe, hats off to you. You are one badass. In fact, all badasses seem positively angelic when compared to you. Be careful, it's okay to have fun within limits, but step on too many toes and your mean streak could land you in trouble one of these days.

If you've scored mostly Bs: You're all sugary sweet. So much so, we're in danger of getting diabetes. Girl, it's not a crime to be naughty once in a while. Nor is it illegal to put your interests first. You should try that sometime. It's good for your soul!

Rinki Tripathi scored mostly Bs.

Chapter 14

BlackBerry Messenger Status: Here's to our (role) model!

So that's how I was cured of the idea of buying and selling question papers. For good.

Really. It was the first time and it was the last time.

Funny thing was, Adit didn't even have to say 'I told you so'. He saw how depressed I was and decided to keep his opinions to himself. And, oh yes, he offered me his hanky when I burst into tears and didn't wince even when I blew heavily into it.

Even when he met Google, Adit was wise enough to hold his fire. I was soooo grateful to him for that. Google looked and felt even more miserable (if that was possible) than me. Would you believe it, he returned our money the very next month?

We wondered how. Not as if it came out of his pocket money. Not as if he had any source of income. It was Big Sis Neha who let the cat out of the bag.

We'd gone over to Google's for a combined study session. (Makes you feel as if we were one studious lot, all these combined study sessions, nah? Trust me, it was more yap yap than mug mug. Once we got all the gossiping out of the way, we settled down to our books.)

'So, did you see all his portraits?' Neha queried, inaugurating the Pre-Study Gossip Session.

'What portraits?' Sudha and I piped up innocently.

Neha gave us a strange look.

'The ones he posed for.'

'Google's a model now?' Robin asked incredulously.

'Before and after ads, I'm sure,' I added with a laugh.

'Oh, so you guys are in the dark? No sh%$. My little bro covers his tracks well.'

'What're you talking about, Neha?'

'Guys, Jugal posed for half my class. Yes posed, as in sat in the same position for hours together till we captured his, er, beauty on the canvas. No, it's not what you're thinking. He did not pose in the nude. We don't do those kind of portraits, for god's sake.'

'Of course,' I said sheepishly.

For those who came in late, Neha was pursuing a Bachelors degree in Fine Arts at a city college.

And for those who know him well enough, Google was a certifiably hyper creature. Restless, fidgety, impatient. Mr Ants in the Pants, no less. For the life of me, I couldn't imagine him sitting still for hours together.

Gosh, we nearly fell off the La-Z-Boy. Google, posing? As a model? Sitting still on his ass just to pay us off? Awwwwww! That was the sweetest, cutest, most generous thing ever.

Right that minute, Google breezed into the room.

'Heyloo, losers! What gives?'

Robin, Sudha and I walked up to him and engulfed him in a bear hug.

'You know, guys, I am the luckiest girl in the world,' I said, after we finally drew apart. 'Really. I may not be the best-looking chick in town . . .'

'I second that,' Google said with a serious nod.

'I may not be the smartest . . .' I continued, grinning like a silly ass.

'Not by a long shot,' Robin agreed wholeheartedly.

'I may not be the sanest . . .' I droned on.

'Not at all,' Sudha concurred.

'But I've the bestest friends in the world. Now don't say anything that'll make me change my mind,' I threatened.

'Let's drink to that!' Google bellowed.

And we did. An unspecified (ahem) number of beer bottles between all of us. Robin was expecting Sriram's call. Sudha had decided (wisely) to stay sober. It was a near perfect evening. If only Adit had been around, it would've been a perfect ten then. No two ways about it.

From Chennai Super Chick's Blog

Is it just me or is the Board Exam tension really on?

Everywhere I look, I see people burying their noses in books.

I mean, it's just the Board Exams. It's not the end of the world.

People say it's important to get good marks or we won't get admission in good colleges.

But helloo, not all of us want to go to the same colleges.

And there are plenty of colleges in the country, right?

I mean, I hope so.

And for creative types like me, what can a college do?

Apart from teaching me how to bunk. Ha ha.

Anyway, I feel you can't teach fashion. You just got to be born with it.

But reading fashion mags definitely helps. Definitely.

And reading fashion blogs too ☺*.*

So don't worry, right until the first bullet is fired and the first exam is overhead, I'll be blogging.

And if you're Miss Mugpots, take a loo break, girl. Read up something else for a change.

You know what they say about all work and no play, right?

Till then, this is your friendly neighbourhood fashionista signing out.

See you soon.

Take care,

Mwaah, mwaaah, mwaah!

Chennai Super Chick

Chapter 15

BlackBerry Messenger Status: It's party time, folks!

Google was throwing a pardy to beat all pardies. His birthday was around the corner. And he was planning to celebrate it in style.

I think the only person more excited than him was ME. He'd made me party planner. Yoohoo! Who cared about being school fashion show coordinator any more? Truth be told, each time I cracked that joke, it felt as if I'd cracked a rib.

Anyway, back to sunnier pastures. I felt like Bittoo and Shruti in *Band Baaja Baraat*, you know. It was a golden opportunity for me. I had to show the world (yet again) that Rinki was the bestest party planner in town. I was armed with my list and good to go.

To-do list:

1. Fix the venue
2. Draw up a list of invitees. Mail the invites
3. Think of idea for invite
4. Get the invite designed
5. Think of overall theme

6. Decide the caterer
7. Decide the items on the menu
8. Fix a DJ (ask him to get the lights, sound box, etc.)
9. Source the décor
10. Order the cake (as per theme)
11. Think of return gifts (if not for everyone, ahem, for close friends ☺)
12. Think of party games
13. Buy the prizes (only first place, too bad about the runners-up)
14. Get him a birthday gift (gosh!)

By the time I finished the list, I was completely stressed out. There were FIFTEEN things to be taken care of. Clearly, planning a party was no party at all.

There was no time to be lost and loads to be done. I was practically a newbie in Chennai. I couldn't possibly do it all. So Santa Rinks decided to rope in her little elves. Enter Neha, Robin and Sudhey.

'Neha, you get the DJ and the caterer.'

'Roger,' Neha yelled, clicking her heels.

'Robin, you're in charge of the cake. And the décor.'

'Aye, aye, Cap'n,' echoed Robin.

'Sudha, think up something for the invite. Ask Neha to design it.'

'But if we do all this, what'll you do, Rinki?' Sudha asked innocently.

'Ladies and gent, meet the brains behind the operation. Rinki T. I'll do the real work. Think up the theme and the invite. Plus the games to go with it.'

Google Search: Birthday party games

'Google, did you draw up the list of people you wanted to invite?'

Google handed me a slip of paper. I was super relieved. Lesser the merrier.

I reached for it but the minute my fingers touched it, it unfurled and unfurled. Finally, it lay there kissing the floor like Princess Kate's wedding entourage!

I was so zapped, I tell you.

'You'd folded the paper several times over,' I accused.

'Never said the job was gonna be easy,' Google said matter-of-factly.

God, I wanted to kill him before his seventeenth birthday.

'Charni, Malini, Medha, Ramya, Sarita, Maya, Vedita, Ayesha,' I reeled names off the list. 'What, no boys?'

'Of course there'll be boys. Your pal, Adit, for one. And me.'

Oh, how lovely.

'How about having it at home?' I asked aloud.

'Chance illa!'

Great, just great.

'Cosmopolitan Club then?'

I'd no personal interest in the place. Not as if I was a member. Not as if it was named after my favourite magazine. Just that Google (and most of Chennai) was crazy about the yummy chicken biryani they served. (No, I wasn't tempted to become a rice eater, not even when the rice was covered with succulent pieces of chicken and mutton).

'I was thinking of Raintree Hotel,' Google's voice cut into my thoughts.

Wait a minute. Did he say Raintree? The Raintree Hotel on Mount Road? It was a star hotel, for crying out loud.

'Wow,' I whistled. 'What's your budget again?'

'No budget. No limit.'

A no-limit budget? I'm sure party planners love hearing that statement, but not *this* party planner. Because right that instant, the scale just went uppppp. From doing an art movie on a shoestring budget, I went straight to directing a 100-crore multi-starrer blockbuster. And that made me wonder. How on earth did KJo do it?

I was busy-busy-busy that week. In the midst of it all, Bhaskar Sir sprang a surprise quiz. And so did Anandi Ma'am. I barely managed to scrape through them. At tuitions, I fared no better. In fact, I was so pooped one Saturday night (all those Bacardi Breezers to keep the butterflies in my belly down), I had to skip class.

I worked before school, after school, during lunch, post dinner. But finally, I cracked it. The theme, that is.

I bounced it off Google, Robin and Sudha at the Backyard.

'What do you think of Pirates and Pixies?'

'It sounds like the sequel to *Pirates of the Caribbean*,' Robin frowned.

'When's it releasing?' Sudha wanted to know.

Jeez.

'Sudhey, it's not a movie, it's the theme for Google's party.'

'Theme as in?'

Was she daft? 'Sudhey, theme as in . . .' I trailed off.

How on earth did one explain a theme?

'Idea, machan. Dress code, décor, cake, invite, all should have the same concept,' Robin explained.

'Why?' Sudha persisted. 'It's just a birthday party.'

'That's where you're wrong, Sudhey. It's much more than just a birthday party. It's a chance to unleash one's creativity, an opportunity to dress up as someone else, someone cooler, someone classier,' I added my two cents.

'Then why dress up as pirates and pixies? Why not people we admire. Like actors? Kollywood stars?'

I opened my mouth to object but Google sprang up like a tightly wound wire and performed a little jig.

'That sounds awesome.' He leaned forward to hug a violently blushing Sudha. 'Ladies, say hello to the theme of Google's Birthday Bash 2011.'

Someone had hijacked my moment of glory yet again. This was not turning out to be a good year. Not in the least.

But very heroically, I didn't let it dampen my spirits. On the contrary, I gave it my best shot.

'Good thought, Sudha. Taking it one step ahead, why don't we call it The Kolaveri Kapers?'

It was my turn to get bear hugged by Google.

The party was a super-duper hit. More like a 100-crore blockbuster.

Oh, yeah. Google didn't know what hit him. We blindfolded him and took him to the banquet hall at Raintree. When the hanky dropped, so did his jaw. It was as if he'd been transported to Kollywood land. Posters of famous K-Town actors and actresses hung from the ceiling. A huge cut-out of a clapboard served as the backdrop.

The stewards were all wearing technicolour shirts and crisp white veshtis.

Robin, the ditcher, was dressed in a pale blue chikan salwar kameez. Said she was playing a 'struggler'. Rrrright!

Sudha came dressed like a village belle. Remember Tabu in *Virasat*? Well, Sudha was dressed like her Kollywood counterpart. A checked *pattu* sari, her hair in two oily plaits with green ribbons, and a huge bindi.

Google, the b'day baby, was dressed like the God of the Silver Screen, Rajini. I must confess he totally looked the part. Resplendent in a shiny golden shirt and an off-white veshti with golden zari that he'd folded to his knees. Supra machan! And yes, he was wearing sunglasses. He'd whip them off his face, juggle them and wear them back every few minutes. Smooth, verrrrry smooth. I was just happy to see that he'd ditched his slogan tees. Really, I'd never tire of pointing out that they were soooo yesterday.

Neha came dressed as an ostrich. Oh sorry, that was Ash in the movie *Endhiran* (for those who don't know, it's the Tamil version of the Hindi film *Robot*). She was wearing a strange multi-coloured skirt, and a steel grey halter top. She'd put her hair up in an elegant (?) updo. It was held in place by strategically located feathers.

Adit came as Surya in *Ghajini*. (The very same movie Aamir remade in Hindi). Minus the biceps, of course. He'd slicked back his hair and was wearing grey pants. He'd rolled up the sleeves of a powder blue shirt. I was kinda impressed. He wasn't the dressing-up type but he'd still taken the effort. Sweet.

As for the belle of the ball, moi, I was wearing a pretty, pretty half-saree à la Shreya in *Sivaji*. It's kind of like a lehenga.

Not that I'd seen too many Tamil movies, but still. I got the silk fabric from Nallis, a green and pink combo with a simple zari border. Mom got her darzi to do a quick job. A simple braid, small *pottu* (bindi, guys), and green glass bangles on the wrist completed the look. A look, I daresay, that was appreciated by one and all. I couldn't wait to upload pix on FB and show them off to Ankita. I knew she'd wholeheartedly approve.

But I wasn't the highlight of the evening. My games were.

I'd written down the names of all Tamil actors and actresses (thank you, Google. Not the person, the search engine) on small chits of paper. I placed them in a small basket at the entrance and stuck them on the back of everyone entering the hall. The first person to guess his identity was the winner.

The second was dumb charades. So I divided the guests into two teams and each enacted a movie. It was howlarious, to say the least! And all of us were rolling on the floor laughing by the time the game ended.

So imagine my surprise when after the party, Google thanked everyone. Neha, Rinki, Robin and Sudha (in that order) for the 'smashingly fab party'. Said it was a joint effort by his 'family and friends' and 'he was so touched at their gesture'. Huh?

I was so zapped. Don't mean to snatch credit from anyone, but IT WAS ME ALL THE WAY. Cross my heart and hope to die. Don't believe me? See for yourself:

Rinki's Efforts:
1. Got the card designed like a clapboard
2. Instructed Adit to ask the DJ to play only Tamil songs

3. Instructed Robin to order 'film reel' shaped cake
4. Asked Robin to decorate the banquet hall at Raintree with Tamil film posters
5. Got sunglasses (cheap ones) as return gifts
6. The crowning glory—the games
7. Made sure a good time was had by all

Neha's Role:
1. Do as Rinki instructed

Robin's Contribution:
1. Do as Rinki suggested

Sudha's Part:
1. Do what Rinki says

I rest my case.

Chapter 16

BlackBerry Messenger Status: With friends like these . . .

It took us one whole month to settle down to our old ways after Mausiji left. It was so weird in the beginning. Don't get me wrong. We were all happy to see the back of Mausiji. In fact, the first few days, all we (Mom and I) could do was crib, crib, crib. But soon, we ran out of steam. There was nothing more to crib about.

Mom and I had been united in our dislike for her. Now, without that binding factor, we drifted apart. And soon, we were picking on each other.

Plus, you know what they say about habits. If you do something for twenty-one days in a row, it becomes a habit. Well, Mom had been fighting with Mausiji for months. Needless to say, she was missing all the action. She needed her daily fix. She needed to pick on someone. And who better than Dad and me?

I was doing the exact same thing with my friends. Of course, I hadn't a clue. Until one fine day Google, Adit and

Robin decided to point it out to me. It took three encounters (one per head) to prompt them into action.

Encounter with Robin
At school

'Rinki, I've a bad feeling about the Pre-Boards. I think I'm going to flunk.'

'Cut it out, Robin,' I snapped.

'No, Rinki, really. Believe me, I haven't even finished my first revision.'

'Oh, spare me! All you mugpots act so helpless and unprepared. In the end, you end up scoring a century.'

'Know something, Rinks? All I've been thinking is when I can see Sriram next. This is so not me. I mean, I should be thinking of books and exams and marks, right?'

'Yeah, Robin. For the next few years of your life, that's all you should think of. Who cares about friends, relationships, boyfriends? It's exams that count.'

'Be serious, Rinks.'

'Oh, I'm very serious, Robin. It's still not too late. Why don't you join my tuition classes? Lord Gaga will be happy to take on enlightened students such as you. Shall I pass on the good news to him? Tell him a gem of a student will be joining us soon?'

'Shut up, Rinks.'

'You know what? I think you should join tuitions. As soon as possible. Don't want to flunk and disappoint your folks right?'

A hurt look crept into Robin's eyes. I knew I'd gone too far even without seeing that look. But she'd so asked for it. Wasn't she fishing for compliments with that sob story of hers? Who in their right minds would believe that Robin wasn't all set to tackle the pesky enemy called Board Exams?

Seconds ticked by. Neither of us attempted to break the chilly silence that'd cropped up.

'Why must you drag my folks into this?' she said at last.

'Well, won't they be disappointed if their darling daughter doesn't hit 90%?'

In reply, Robin picked up her school bag and turned on her heel.

Rendezvous with Google
At the Backyard

'Bye, Google,' I said, gulping down my coffee. 'It's getting late. I've got be home. Got some studying to do. Pre-Boards are just around the corner and . . .'

I shut up abruptly. Gosh, I sounded just like Robin. Guilt reared its ugly head and suddenly, I felt sick to the stomach.

'Awww, Rinki!' Google drawled, waving his right hand in air. 'I think you're turning into a big bore.'

I chewed on my bottom lip. I should've let it pass. But I guess I was too tuned into the fighting mode.

'What do you mean?' I asked, a big frown on my face. I crossed my arms over my chest and waited for the answer I knew would come.

'I don't know. You're different somehow.'

'Different? How?'

I was playing a cat and mouse game. I knew what was coming but instead of deflecting it, I wanted to draw it out sooner. I was spoiling for a fight for sure.

'You're not the Rinki I used to know.'

'I'm not,' I said coldly.

'No! Old Rinki used to be so much fun. Naughty and mischievous . . .'

'They mean the same thing,' I cut in.

'What?'

'Naughty and mischievous. They mean the same thing. They are synonyms,' I added for good measure.

'See, that's exactly what I mean. Now, you spout all these big words.'

'Synonym is a big word only to a dunce.'

'There, that's another one. Dunce.'

I sighed. I was fighting a losing battle.

'Hmm, back to what I was saying. Rinks, you are boring. All you seem to do is study, study, study.'

'Well, I'm sorry to disappoint you, Mr Jugal Varma.'

'Who?' For a second, Google was genuinely muddled up.

See, that's what happens when you stick with your pet name.

I continued as if his confusion hadn't registered. 'I'm sorry I don't live up to your high standards. It's my fault. You see, some of us have to study to get ahead in life. Unlike you, we can't afford to buy our degree, buy the question paper, etc., etc.'

Google looked as if I'd slapped him on the face with a stinking wet fish.

He stared at me for one whole minute and swayed lightly on his feet. Suddenly, I was worried. What if he jumped off the ledge? Surely, I hadn't upset him so much with my jab about money? Much to my (short-lived) relief, he proceeded to pick himself up, and ambled away. Leaving me alone on the rooftop, with empty coffee mugs and a half-finished packet of chips lying around me.

Tête-à-tête with Adit
At tuitions

'Rinki, did you finish the homework Pragash Sir gave us?'

I ignored Adit's query, pretending to pack my bag. I stuffed the books into the bag ever so slowly, without raising my eyes to meet his.

'Rinki, I'm asking you something.'

'Why?'

Adit was taken aback. Both by my question and the sharp tone in which I uttered it.

'What do you mean "why"?'

'When you know the answer, why bother?'

'Rinki, what're you talking about? I do not know the answer. That's why I'm asking.'

'You do know the answer,' I spat out. 'You know I haven't done the homework. You're just taunting me.'

'Why would I do that, Rinki?' Adit asked, throwing his hands up in exasperation.

'Because you want to prove what a horrible student I am,' I choked out the words. My tears were threatening to spill on to my face.

'Why would I do something like that?'

'Because you are mean. You always want to prove how superior you are and . . . and . . . you love showing off . . . and . . . and putting me down,' I exploded.

'Are you done listing out my virtues?' Adit asked after a

painful minute of eerie silence. Swiftly followed by a full-blown slanging match. Slanging matches were becoming a permanent feature of my life.

I was so exhausted at the end of it, I had to sit down on the pavement to catch my breath.

Adit picked up his books and walked over to his pink Scooty. The other students hadn't come out yet. I found myself standing on the road all alone. It wasn't as if I felt particularly lonely or anything. Just that I was totally overwhelmed by everything around me. Tears came quick and fast.

I cried and cried and cried till a small crowd of curious onlookers gathered around me. The guy from the tea stall, the mechanic from the car workshop next door, even a pot-bellied uncle who lived across the street, all gaped at me, wondering what brought it on and what they could do to stop it.

Finally, the tea-stall owner could hold himself back no longer. He cleared his throat but I kept crying my guts out. At long last, when I met his eyes, he handed me a small cup of tea. He even refused to accept any payment.

That small act of kindness made me realize how nasty I'd been. To my friends. To the most special people in my life. And that brought on a fresh bout of tears.

'*Romba romba thanks*,' I mumbled before rushing home. That tuition class I was better off bunking.

I passed that entire weekend in utmost misery. It was official. I was friendless.

Rinki Tripathi blocked 3 friends from her Facebook Friend List.

From Chennai Super Chick's blog

Hey, all you beautiful people out there!

Especially the ones who read my blog ☺

This is a very important, shoot-a-printout-and-keep-it-under-your-pillow-important, post.

The pearls of wisdom I'm about to share right now, you'll thank me for them later. Trust me.

It's this: The FIVE must-haves in any fashionista's wardrobe.

Just five, you may ask. Well, it is not the quantity of your possessions, it's the quality. Always the quality.

1. *A white shirt. Classic. Beautiful. Effortlessly chic. Just remember to dry-clean after each use.*
2. *A well-fitted pair of denims. You can hold on to them forever. Don't compromise on the brand. If you pinch pennies on this one, you'll live to regret it.*
3. *An LBD. Little Black Dress. It's such a beauty. And best of all, it never goes out of style. A good investment, no?*
4. *Pretty accessories. Read any fashion mag. Talk to a stylist. Corner any fashion guru. And they'll give you one piece of advice: Accessorize. Belts, shoes, handbags, beads, hairbands, bracelets, you name it.*
5. *A good make-up kit. Again, buy only the best brands. Nothing but the best for your skin, right?*

Now, go, shoot that printout. And yes, you're most welcome. Have fun over the weekend.

Much love,

CSC

Chapter 17

BlackBerry Messenger Status: Friendship means always having to say sorry.

I didn't hear from my wolf pack for two whole days. That made for an extremely (to the power of hundred) horrible weekend.

Mom and Dad were getting along better. Guess they were more used to sharing space. Watching them, I really wanted to kick myself for giving my friends grief. If my parents could be civil and friendly, why couldn't I? It was just that the pressure of exams, parents, life, everything had got to me. I needed to vent. And bad.

So I decided to channel all my anger and put it to good use. I hit the books with a vengeance and spent all afternoon studying. Yes, you heard me right. Sure, the thoughts of my friends kept haunting me but I refused to get distracted. I gave my Business Studies textbook a good read.

I mean, what else could I do? I didn't want to go out with Mom, and Dad couldn't take me along to his office. And I very well couldn't go anywhere alone. (Have a coffee/watch a movie all by myself! How sad was that?)

The other option was out of the question. I so didn't want to call up my friends and apologize. Sure, I was wrong. But it wasn't as if they were Mother Teresa, Nelson Mandela and Mahatma Gandhi. If they needed me, they'd say sorry. But as the weekend flew by and no call came, I realized something: You could never rely on friends.

I stuck to that uncomfy thought till Saturday evening. Then the phone rang.

'Hello?' I said, listlessly.

'Hi.'

My heart stopped. It was Adit.

'I was thinking of taking a break from studying this evening. Got a couple of DVDs. Romcoms, horror, thrillers. Interested?'

Ohmyyygosh. Adit! Sweet Adit! Here I was, cursing him, and he was making up with me.

'Yes,' I said gruffly.

'Will ask Google to pick you up.'

Hang on. Did he just say Google? I thought they couldn't stand each other. What was Adit doing inviting Google over to his place? Had the world gone all topsy-turvy in the last two days? Had they kissed (strictly in a manner of speaking) and made up? Had Jennifer and Angelina made up too?

I nixed all those nagging questions that sprang to mind and grunted in reply.

Hanging up quickly, I made a beeline for my room. I yanked open my cupboard and decided to go all out. I pulled on my favourite pair of blue jeans (low waist, tapered leg, super

flattering) and dug around till I found my sleeveless white vest.
I threw on a cute shrug over it. A coat of gloss, a hint of kohl,
a dab of perfume on my wrists, and I was ready to go.

'Mom, Dad, going out for a couple of hours,' I knocked
on their door and called out.

'Where? With whom?' That was Dad.

'Oh, you poor thing, holed up in your room studying for
two days. Go, go, have fun.' That was Mom.

'We should've found out where she was going and with
whom,' I heard Dad say.

'Oh, she hangs out only with Robin and Sudha. She doesn't
have any other friends.'

Wow, how well Mom knew me. Trouble was, after
those huge rows, I wasn't sure if I'd still have those same
old friends.

I walked till the main gate and sure enough, Google was
waiting in his car. I reached for the passenger door but there
was someone sitting there. Robin! Wow, so all my friends were
best friends with each other now. Thick as thieves.

Even without me in the picture, I thought, thoroughly
annoyed.

'Hi,' Google and Robin chorused.

'Hi!' I said extra brightly. With about the same amount
of fake enthusiasm I usually reserved for acquaintances and
non-friends. We drove ahead in silence.

'Wonder if Sudha's reached,' Robin said to Google.

'Why don't you call her?' he replied. 'I'm sure she has a
cell. In this day and age, who doesn't?'

Robin shot him a warning look.

Google gave me a pitying look and mumbled, 'Oh, I forgot.'

I mean, they were actually having a conversation AND not bothering to include me. I wanted to scream and jump out of the car. I was so mad at them.

Right there and then, I vowed not to utter a word for the rest of the evening. Not that they tried making a conversation with me either. At least, no genuine effort.

'Where are we picking Adit from?' I began, treating my resolve like a New Year resolution.

'Near Adit's place. Pasumpon Muthuramalinga Thevar Salai,' Robin supplied. 'Know the area?'

Oh, yeah, I went to Pasupo . . . whatever road every day of my life.

Google braked in front of a house and in my hurry to jump out of the car, I opened the door while the car was still moving.

'What's wrong with you?' Google yelled.

That was all I could take. I broke my vow with a loud, 'What's wrong with you?'

'Are you crazy, jumping off the car like that?'

'You're crazy, driving the car like that,' I shouted back.

'Guys, please . . .' began Robin.

'Shuuttttuppp Robin,' Google and I yelled in unison.

Adit came running out of his house.

'Guys, guys, what's going on?'

'I told you, Rinki's got an attitude problem,' Google said to no one in particular.

Gosh, that hurt.

'What???' I bellowed. 'HOW DARE YOU?'

How dare they discuss me behind my back? They knew each other because of me. BECAUSE OF ME. Had I known they'd end up ganging up against me, I would've never, ever introduced them.

'How dare you talk about me behind my back?' I hollered.

'Rinki, please calm down,' Robin spoke up, looking hugely troubled. 'It's not like that.'

'So you haven't been talking about me behind my back?' I challenged.

Robin bit her lip.

'We're worried about you, Rinks,' she mumbled.

'I'm worried about you guys. You seem to be losing it big time,' I railed.

'Why don't we do this inside?' Adit cajoled, casting an uncomfortable glance around him.

Reluctantly, we complied. (Let it be said, no neighbours were harmed in the making of the fight.)

I pushed past Adit and stomped in.

What I saw inside completely took my breath away. The walls were covered with paintings—abstracts, portraits, landscapes and what not. I had been to Adit's place once earlier, but hadn't seen the living room.

'Awesome,' Robin breathed.

'My sister's work,' Adit said proudly. 'She's a Fine Arts student.'

'Hey, my sister's doing Fine Arts too, machan,' Google piped in.

'Stella Maris?'

'Stella Maris,' Google nodded.

'What a small world. What's your sister's name?'

'Neha.'

'Okay, I'll ask Anu if she knows her.'

That was one thing I didn't get about Chennai. Everyone seemed to know everyone. So many schools, so many colleges, so many communities, so many social circles. And yet, somehow, everything and everyone was linked. Crazzzzzy. That would never happen in Delhi. Talk about small cities, I thought uncharitably.

'Make yourselves comfy, guys. I'll get you all something to drink.'

'Why don't I help you?' Robin offered.

'Hey, chill. Don't be so formal.'

'Good thing my folks aren't home or they would've fainted seeing you guys fight,' Adit said, placing a tray laden with banana chips, *murukku* and tall glasses of *yellaneer* (tender coconut water) on the centre table.

One look at those no-one-can-eat-just-one banana chips and I almost drooled. Given my weight, I made a sensible decision. I reached for the glass of coconut water and drained its contents in one swift swig.

'Wow, you must be really thirsty. Another one?'

I shook my head.

'Sorry, Google. Liquor is banned in my house.'

'No probs, Dude. Coconut water is good. Next time I'll just remember to carry a vodka miniature with me!'

Adit laughed.

This was turning out to be a disaster. I felt as if I was in a daze. Adit and Google were joking around like old friends. And suddenly, I felt insecure, like an outsider. What if everyone continued meeting each other and cut me off completely? I'd be friendless all over again. Just when I'd settled down in Chennai, started thinking of it as home. Yes, really.

'So, Rinki, we all wanted to talk to you,' Adit began.

I raised my eyebrows.

'I thought we were going to watch movies.'

'We will. Just as soon as we get this silly quarrel out of the way.'

Adit glanced at Robin.

'Rinks, we know you've been through a lot these last few months. Sharing your roof with a dragon . . .' she spoke up.

Dragon? Hmm. Come to think of it, the word was so apt for Mausiji.

'. . . Missing your dad . . .'

Yeah, kinda. He does have a calming presence. Ask Mom.

'. . . Getting into Princy's bad books . . .'

Hey, at least I was consistent.

'. . . Not getting selected as fashion show coordinator . . .'

Well, shit happens. But I couldn't kid myself any longer. My life was beginning to sound like one giant mess.

'. . . Faring badly at school . . .'

'Okay, stop, stop, where's this leading . . .' I cut in.

Robin let out a long sigh.

'We just want to say, we understand. We know you've not had it easy. We just want to be there for you,' Adit finished.

He then elbowed Google, who pursed his lips. Adit kicked him under the table.

Google piped up, 'Ouch! I mean, yeah, me too.'

I surveyed the painting on the wall. It was of a little baby, surrounded by four little angels. Wasn't that cosy, being watched over by four angels, no less?

For some reason, that made me cry. My friends weren't finding faults with me. They weren't cutting me out of their lives. They were just saying they cared. I was soooo touched. I wanted to say thank you. But that would've sounded so formal, no? After all, you can't thank friends for being friends, can you?

All three of my angels reached out and covered my hand with theirs.

The doorbell rang.

Sudha breezed in. 'Hey, what did I miss?'

Well, where do I start. I'll spare all the mushy details of that evening. Let me just say that we spent the rest of it watching those Tamil flicks Adit had rented out for us.

And they were brilliant. Most had superheroes (as opposed to just heroes) in the lead. They could stop trains with their will power, catch flying bullets and hurl them back at the bad guys. And in one bizarre case, even chew on them and spit them out! We had a super-duper time.

When my angels finally dropped me home, I felt twenty kilograms lighter.

Rinki Tripathi unblocked 3 friends on Facebook.

Sunday had another pleasant surprise in store. Tuitions were cancelled. Pragash Sir was down with diarrhoea. Ha ha. Or should that be ga ga.

'Guess it's back to the pavilion,' I chirped as Adit and I walked out of class.

'Unless,' Adit hesitated. 'You want to do something.'

'Oh, yeah! I want to run home. Hit the bed. Catch up on my beauty sleep.'

'No, no, I meant, with me,' Adit said quietly, his face turning a weird shade of crimson.

Wait a minute. He was asking me out? Well, I never!

'Hmm . . . what did you have in mind?' I asked cautiously.

Where could we go at six o'clock in the morning? Jogging on Marina Beach?

'Murugan Idly Shop.'

So that's where.

'Okay,' I shrugged.

I mean, how dangerous could sharing idlis be?

Adit stepped back politely and gestured at his pink Scooty. 'After you.'

Great.

I swung a leg over it and sidled to the back.

'Sorry, I don't have a spare helmet.'

I checked my hair out in the rearview mirror and muttered, 'I'm not sorry at all.'

I was wearing horrible tuition gear. My hair was flat. I looked as if I'd just dragged myself out of bed. I mean, I had. Luckily, I'd taken a shower and used generous pumps of deodorant.

Some date.

But I forgot all my misgivings at Murugan Idly Shop.

'Do you like idlis?' Adit asked, pulling a chair out for me.

Awww.

'Sure do.'

'And dosas?'

'Yup.'

'And . . .'

I held up a hand. 'Adit, as long as it's tasty, I'll eat anything.'

Adit's face broke into a huge smile.

'Oh, it's very tasty. Trust me, you won't be disappointed,' he said, placing the order.

And I wasn't.

The idlis were white and soft as a Johnson baby's bottom. And the dosas about as 'kadak' (crisp) as Mrs Verghese. The sambhar was as spicy as Ankita's tongue, and the chutney as tangy as Google's ideas.

Google! The thought of him made me guilty. Hey, it wasn't as if I was cheating on him. I. Was. Not. He was not my boyfriend. He. Was. Not.

Two dates did not a boyfriend make. Besides, this was not a date. Just as the thought popped into my head, the waiter popped up with the tab. Adit promptly settled it, leaving me decidedly unsettled.

'Shall I drop you home?' Adit asked me as the waiter cleared away our almost-licked-dry banana leaves.

'Better if I rick it up. My parents might have a fit if they see me on the bike with you.'

'With me?'

'With any boy.'

'So you don't generally go out with boys?' Adit asked, a sympathetic look on his face.

Uh, oh.

'You broke a rule for me?' Adit went on. 'Wouldn't want to get you into trouble . . .'

I couldn't keep mum any longer.

'Adit, wait. It's not as if I don't go out with boys. I do. I just make sure my parents don't know about it.'

'So you lie to them.' Adit looked distinctly uncomfortable with the whole lying business.

Not as if I could help it.

'Yes, by omission mostly,' I replied. 'I usually say I'm spending the night at a friend's. Or say I'm meeting the girls for dinner. Something like that.'

'Won't it be easier to tell them the truth?'

'No!' I said sharply. 'You don't know my folks. If they found out I was dating guys, they'd ground me for life.'

'You're dating guys?' Adit repeated, his eyebrows shooting up in surprise.

'Just you. And Google.'

A horrified expression came over Adit's face. 'Google?'

'He didn't tell you?' I couldn't resist asking. 'I thought you guys were pally.'

'Well, we just got to know each other. He's an okay guy. Lent me his DVDs, you know.'

That explained the brotherhood. Gosh, boys were so silly.

'I'm sorry, Rinki. Had I known . . .'

'You wouldn't have asked me to have idlis with you?' I retorted before he could finish. 'Adit, you're being silly. Google and I are not going around. I'm sure he won't have a problem.'

'I hope so.'

On to explaining my casual dating stance to Google. Ughh. A-W-K-W-A-R-D. But some things just have to be done.

I picked up my landline and dialled Google the minute I reached home.

'Who? What?' came his groggy voice.

'Googs, it's me, Rinki.'

'Rinki? Are you out of your f*^%ing mind? Why're you calling me in the middle of the night?'

'It's eight in the morning.'

'Same thing. And hey, it's Sunday! I have the official licence to sleep. Okay? All right? Fine?'

'Whatever,' I mumbled under my breath.

'Can I go back to sleep now? Or do I've to ask my girlfriend's permission for that too?' he grumbled.

Oh, shoot.

'Actually, Google, I was calling about that,' I said, taking a deep breath. 'Just wanted to clarify something with you. Googs, I'm so sorry if I gave you that impression but I'm not your girlfriend.'

'Huh? Why not?' Google sounded wide awake now.

'Because . . . I'm not,' I said desperately.

'But you went out with me twice, Rinki.'

'I also went out with Adit,' I quickly put in. 'Does that make me his girlfriend too?'

'You what? When? Why?' Google bellowed. I could half imagine him jumping on his bed in sheer agitation.

'Google, calm down please. We just went for breakfast. To Murugan Idly Shop.'

'That dog! That snake! I thought he was my friend! I'm going to kill him!'

'Googs, puhleeeeze! Stop being so melodramatic. It was just a casual outing.'

'With Adit?'

'With both of you. You're my closest friends. Why can't I hang out with both of you?'

'Because you can't. It won't be right,' Google whined.

'Says who? There are no rules. It's we who get to decide. If it feels right, it's right. Google? Are you listening? Hey, you there?'

There was a long pause.

'Fine, Rinki. Do what you want!' Google said abruptly.

He hung up before I could say another word.

Google was majorly pissed with me. Guess Adit wasn't too happy with the situation either. Gawd, I wish there was something I could do. Apart from dating only one of them, that is. Good thing, none of us had the luxury of breaking our heads over it. Soon, the terror of Board Exams infiltrated our minds. And matters of the heart were put on the back burner.

Rinki Tripathi is taking an online quiz on Teenz Forever

Quiz #999. Lucky Fellow or Poor Thing: How lucky are you?

1. Have you ever found a 1,000-rupee note lying on the ground?
   a. Only if I've dropped it
   b. Why not? Finders keepers, right?

2. Ever found coins in old purses, sofa sets, pockets?
   a. Sometimes I feel my pockets have holes in them
   b. Digging a coin out of my sofa even as I type this

3. Ever gone into an examination hall unprepared only to find the paper cancelled?
   a. That happens in real life too?
   b. Yes, in IX grade

4. Do you get unexpected gifts from friends and family?
   a. I don't even get the expected ones
   b. Doesn't everyone?

5. Your name is mostly prefixed with:
   a. Loser
   b. Lucky

If you've scored mostly As: Hate to break this to you, but you're not lucky. Anything but. The stars are so not in your favour. In fact, they might be conspiring against you even as we speak. It's kinda sad but there it is. Luckily (er, pardon the pun) for you, these things aren't permanent. Who knows you may wake up tomorrow and find out that you've won the lottery? Not THE lottery, maybe the last prize or something. So don't give up hope just yet.

If you've scored mostly Bs: Don't we all just hate your guts! You're one lucky devil. Oh, yeah! Looks like nothing can keep you down. Your run of good luck defies earthly explanation. Even in cases where you ought to get your ass kicked, you don't. Enjoy it while it lasts, we say.

Rinki Tripathi scored mostly As.

From Chennai Super Chick's Blog

The long overdue Chennai vs Delhi match finally happened.

> *No, no, you cricket crazies, not an IPL match.*

> *A fair and square comparison between the two lovely metros. Who won? Aiyyooo, read on to find out.*

Chennai vs Delhi
Round One

In Delhi, if the pollution doesn't kill you, the distances will.

> *Out here in Chennai, people frequently refer to places that take twenty minutes to reach as 'romba far'.*

> *Chennai 1 Delhi 0*

Round Two

In Delhi, discos and pubs are open till wee hours of the morning.

In Chennai, they take the last order for food and drinks at, hold your breath, 10.30 pm

Chennai 1 Delhi 1

Round Three

But if you're a girl in Delhi, and you take advantage of the above rule, you've high chances of getting raped/molested/abducted.

In Chennai, all the rapists/molesters/abductors are home after 10.30 (to open their own alcohol bottles, no doubt)

Chennai 2 Delhi 1

Round Four

In Delhi, cinema tickets cost rupees 250 and above. And if it's the opening weekend, god help you. (Just add the cost of the popcorn and colas and puffs and yes, parking tickets in the malls.)

In Chennai, ticket prices cannot exceed rupees 120. Any movie, any day of the week, any show.

Chennai 3 Delhi 1

Round Five

Shopping in Delhi is awesome.

What? Shopping in Chennai? Ha ha.

Chennai 3 Delhi 2

Round Six

Delhi food—black dal at Pandara Road, strawberry milk at Keventers, bread pakora at Kamla Nagar—slurp! I've put on a kilogram just thinking about it all.

Chennai food—crisp dosas at Sarvana Bhawan, idlis at Murugan Idly, thaali at Amravati—OMG, add another kilogram to that
  Tie! One point to each team!
  Chennai 4 Delhi 3

Round Seven
Delhi—Ankita
  Chennai—Robin, Google, Adit, Sudha
  Tie! One point to each team! (This is becoming like a Federer–Nadal match, guys.)
  Chennai 5 Delhi 4

Round Eight
Delhi—Mausiji's official residence
  Chennai—No Mausiji (yipeee!)
  Chennai 6 Delhi 4

Round Nine
Public Transport in Delhi can be used by the public
  Public Transport in Chennai? If you're a girl travelling on a bus, shudder! As for autos, do I need to add more?
  Chennai 6 Delhi 5

Round Ten (Last round, what say?)
Delhi has Daredevil Gautam Gambhir
  But Chennai has many Super Kings. Mahi, Raina, Vijay
  2 points (one bonus) to Team Chennai
  Chennai 8 Delhi 5

Final Results: Chennai 8 Delhi 5

*OHMYYYGOOOOD, a clean sweep for Chennai! Who'd have thought!
An ex-Dilliwalli like moi giving the prize and the heart away to
Namma Chennai? Woooow, when did that happen? Sigh. Something
like lau, no? You never know when it sneaks up on you. And before you
know it, you're head over heels in luuuurvve.*

Think about it, guys.
XOXOXO
Chennai Super Chick

Rinki Tripathi is taking an online quiz on Teenz Forever

Quiz #1001: Are you an Online Quiz (OQ) Addict?
1. Are you taking this online quiz?
    a. Duh, yeah
    b. Not really, just skimming through

2. How many OQ have you taken in this lifetime?
    a. Stopped counting after 500
    b. This is my first one

3. The moment you finish an OQ, you're itching to do another. Right?
    a. 'You mindreader, you'
    b. Thanks but no thanks, this one was tiresome enough

4. If you don't agree with the results of an OQ, you:
    a. Take it again and again till the results agree with you
    b. Snap the comp shut in irritation

5. Do friends and family know about your OQ habit?
   a. No! It's my guilty secret
   b. Yeah, sure, I don't see why not

If you've scored mostly As: Boy, you've got a bad case of addiction. Get off the comp, now! Why're you reading the next para, I said NOWWWW!

If you've scored mostly Bs: There's hope for you yet.

Rinki Tripathi scored mostly As.

Chapter 18

BlackBerry Messenger Status: Chilling sent a chill down my spine.

Subject: Maths
Preparation Level: 4/10
Anxiety Level: 10/10

I hate figures. Both the ones that go 36-24-36 and the ones that go 1-2-3. But as the ancient Chinese saying goes, you cannot postpone bad luck for too long. My bad luck had finally arrived. In the form of Board Exams. Boo hoo. Sob. Sob.

I don't know about you, but if someone volunteers to share good news and bad news, I always, always opt for good news. Like if I'm going in for the buffet, I eat the worst item last.

So imagine my plight when the exam timetable came and I saw Business Math topping the list! What a way to kick-start the sorry event.

But like Google's T-shirt said, what cannot be cured has to be insured. Sadly enough, I hadn't. Insured myself by studying hard, that is.

Too late.

I was a nervous wreck the week leading to the paper. Mom made me copious cups of coffee every night, in the hope that I'd burn some midnight oil. But the minute she was out of the door, my head would drop on the book. It'd stay that way till morning, when Mom came in with my milk cuppa.

Robin was not doing any better. According to reports (sent by Sudha, who else) she was losing over 100 strands of hair a day. Last count: 120. Sure shot sign of stress. Doctor Rinks advised Robin to start popping Becosule tablets. Gosh, some people don't have their priorities right. I mean, it's okay to lose a few marks here and there, but hair? Now that's something that just doesn't grow back in a hurry.

Sudha wasn't faring very well in the tackle stress department either. According to reports (sent by Robin, who else) she spent her evenings running around the dining table, claiming she'd wasted the entire day.

No clue how Adit was doing. There was no way of finding out. He was super paranoid. Which meant, answering phone calls, reading the paper, watching TV (and I'm guessing, going to the loo) were all ruled out during the week. He'd cut off his Tata Sky connection. In all probability, his Airtel connection would soon follow suit.

Knowing Google, he must have been acting as if he was going for a picnic on Friday.

When Freaky Friday finally rolled by, I prayed to every single god known to mankind. And then it was on to Math Madness.

Bottomline: The paper sprang no surprises. Anyone who'd slogged over the textbooks and old question papers (unlike me) could've cracked it.

Subject: Business Studies
Preparation Level: 7/10
Anxiety Level: 3/10

I was kind of ready for BS. (Not to be confused with the other, more common full form of BS.)

Didn't feel the need or desperation to mug. I mean, I'd practically applied every (okay, some) aspect of it in my daily life. Like the chapter on organizing and planning. Heylooo, I did that on a regular basis what with my party-throwing skills. After English, it was the only paper I had a decent feeling about.

Unfortunately, so did the cheaters. The day before the BS exam, newspapers dropped the bombshell: CBSE question paper leaked.

Bottomline: The paper was postponed, right to the very end.

P.S. When we reached there, the BS paper turned out pretty okay. Like an Akshay Kumar movie. I didn't go in with too many expectations, so I wasn't really disappointed.

Subject: Auditing
Preparation Level: 6/10
Anxiety Level: 4/10

I was so not prepared for the Auditing paper. I mean, sure, I knew it was going to come up. But not so soon. Not just yet. Those cheating scoundrels had really pulled the rug from under my feet.

I called Robin for a much-needed combined study session, but she refused outright. Said she didn't want to lose time travelling. She was acting like a complete psycho. Lose time, my foot. What about the knowledge she'd gain?

Although, to be fair, she wouldn't gain much knowledge studying with me. Unless it was about fashion.

Ooh, fashion. The word made me weep. It'd been a whole month since I'd leafed through a fashion mag. Mom had made sure of that. I had to make do with my old stash that I kept in a 'safe location' in my room. Sorry, I cannot jinx it by revealing it.

Subject: English
Preparation Level: 100/10
Anxiety Level: 0/10

We got one week off, one whole week, for the English paper! I tell you, those guys who set the dates (and the question papers) have one sick sense of humour.

I mean, with such a long break and such a simple paper ahead, the entire serious exam mood dissipated.

I almost went back to my wild ways. I watched back-to-back episodes of *The Big Bang Theory*, watched *Batman Begins* online for the zillionth time and made a flying visit on FB. Strictly under invisible mode. One never knew when Mom and Mausiji were up to their online expeditions. Eww.

Bottomline: I could've aced the paper in my sleep.

Subject: Accountancy
Preparation Level: Couldn't care less
Anxiety Level: Beyond all those emotions

I was sooo sick of the whole exam tension that I couldn't bring myself to feel anything. I felt numb, dazed and soo tired. In fact, I wanted to join Mom on one of her 'full body massage' sprees. Of course, asking for some free time (read 'me time') during the exams is like asking for parole after spending just a week in jail. So I bore my burden with a grimace. My friends were either:

AWOL (Absent Without Leave)—Sudha
MIA (Missing In Action)—Robin
RIP (Revising in Peace)—Adit

Google? Well, he just could not be trusted at a time like this. He could mess with your head. Just one phrase, one look, and it would be all over. You'd never look at your books the same way. You simply wouldn't feel like it. No, I couldn't afford to take that risk.

I had to chill. I had to unwind. I had to loosen all those taut muscles in my body which were coiled like serpents ready to strike. I had to organize a spa theme private party just for poor li'l me. Since the customer couldn't go to the spa, the spa had to come to the customer. I got into action.

THINGS NEEDED FOR SPA

1. Agarbattis. Check. Told Mom I was going to offer special prayers to god. She handed me a whole bunch she'd just got from the Auroville store at KNK Road. Mmm, divine.
2. Jasmine (mallipoo) flowers. Check. Made a deal with my maid Rakamma. She agreed to go without her mallipoo gajra for a day.
3. Fluffy bath towels. Pinched from Mom's linen closet. She hardly ever opened it. Like many other domains, it came under the jurisdiction of the hired help.
4. Tub with warm water. Check.

5. Face pack. Check. Besan (gram flour) and a pinch (only a pinch) of turmeric from the kitchen. Cup of milk from the fridge.
6. Aromatherapy candles. Check. Had been saving this awesome Marks and Spencer set Ankita had gifted me.
7. Scented oils. Check. Helped myself to some jars in Mom's bathroom cabinet.
8. Bacardi Breezer. Check. This was a tricky one. Hid one in the freezer for a little under an hour and it was good to go.
9. Bathrobe. Check. Rinki's own.
10. Cuban cigar. Check. Flicked from Ankita's dad. Saved for special occasions / emergency situations such as these.
11. Fashion magazines. Check. Not the latest issues, only old ones stashed away but still.
12. Soft, lilting music. Check. Rinki's own.
13. Right day and time. Check. Tonight. Mom and Dad were going to be away at their friend's party. They wouldn't be home until much later. Purrfect. Remember my cat away, mouse at play theory?

I really had to thank the guy who wrote my business studies textbook. Without his help and in-depth knowledge, I couldn't have organized an event of this magnitude. Indeed, a lot of thinking and planning and research had gone into the spa night. I was going to miss my friends but hey, you can't have everything, right?

So, there I was, bang in the middle of the night (and ahem, the exam week) lounging in my bathrobe. All around me candles flickered, the scent of agarbattis was in the air. My face pack had solidified nicely (not so gooey that it would run, not so thick that I'd have to scrape it off with a knife). A copy of *Cosmo* lay open in my lap, music wafted out of my PC speakers. The Breezer bottle was in my left hand, the Cuban cigar in my right, my feet were dipped in a tub of warm water. And that's how Mom and Dad found me.

Blooddddddy hell! I hadn't heard or seen a thing. Not when the key turned in the lock of the main door, not when the handle of my room door turned, not when they sauntered in, eager to share the spoils of that evening. Only when Mom dropped the tin of cookies she'd won in tambola, did I look up.*

*The ensuing conversation has been deleted in Rinki's personal interest.

Chapter 19

BlackBerry Messenger Status: Yoohoooooo! Board Exams are over! My life is just getting started!

You know those old Hindi movies, where blind old ladies in pristine white miraculously get their eyesight back and go exclaiming, 'I can see! I can see everything'?

Well, on 31 March 2012, I felt exactly like that.

Really. I wanted to wrap a flag of India around myself and streak (pun unintended) through the streets of Chennai proclaiming, 'I'm free! I'm free!'

Because, as of 31 March 2012, I WAS FREE.

Free to breathe.

Free to live.

Free to chill.

Free to dance.

Free to sing.

Free to pardyyyy.

Free to spend six hours straight on FB.

Free to watch TV all night.

Free to daydream.

Free to shop.

Free to sell my books to some soon-to-be XII grader. And blow the cash on a cool outfit.

The monkey was off my back. The dagger hovering over my head had finally been lifted. The ghost of Board Exams had been laid to rest.

But before I say goodbye, I think I need to tell you what happened to all the supporting characters. Like they do in the movies just before the end credits roll.

Let's start with Anks, the first among equals BFF. She passed. Missed first class by a whisker. But Anks being Anks, she didn't take it to heart. To quote her, 'Percentages are like pimples. You can't do shit about them.'

As for Robin, she scored a cool 85%. In the over-studious world, however, that's a cause for mourning. She'd missed the magical 90-mark by far. (Am rolling my eyes here). I tried drilling some sense into her but to no avail. It took a surprise visit by Sriram Anna (mine not hers) to pull her out of the doldrums. Last checked, Robin was doing fine and was looking forward to applying to *all* city colleges Why? In her words, 'With just 85%, you never know.'

Yeah, so, Adit passed with flying colours. Literally. A super 91%. He was riding back on his pink Scooty to share the good news with his folk. In his excitement, he accelerated when he should've braked; the bike spun around, and he went flying. But no harm done. Thanks to the helmet, he escaped with minor injuries, and a strong warning from his sister. (It was her bike, after all.)

Google passed too. To this day, he refuses to share the secret. Was it last minute studying? Was it the constant nagging? By friends and family alike? Or did he just pay someone somewhere a sum he couldn't refuse to 'chase' his paper? Sigh. I shall never know. What I do know is that Google is beyond all this. Things that concern/trouble/affect normal teens don't apply to him. Google is beyond natural catastrophes, man-made calamities, self-inflicted disasters. He's a cockroach, that boy. Mark my words. He'd survive it all.

Sudha scored a respectable 71%. ('After studying only this much, I got 71%. Imagine if I'd studied more,' she remarked later). I simply cannot imagine what stopped her.

What about ME? Ha ha ha. Whatte joke. Really. You've got to be kidding! My weight and my XII-grade percentage are the two things in life I'll NEVER share. EVER.

All I can say is, I've been honourably discharged from the military camp called school.

Soon, I'm going to be eighteen. Eighteen. Awesome, right?

Rinki T is going to be cooler than ever. If that's possible. Life's going to rock. Big time.

Gosh, I can hardly wait.

Sheena Tripathi posted on Rinki Tripathi's wall: 61% in Board Exams! So proud of you, Rinki, my darling daughter!
Meenkashi Chaturvedi commented on Sheena's post: 61? Same as her weight? Harrumph.

Read More in This Series

Sweet Sixteen (Yeah, right!)

Vibha Batra

From Oye to Aiyyo, from dahi bhallas to bisi bele, from rajma to rasam, watch Rinki's life take one big 360 degree skid

Vannakam. It's the summer of 2010 and sixteen-year-old Rinki Tripathi has just been sentenced. To a life in Chennai. She is supposed to say goodbye to her BFF, her beloved hometown Dilli, basically her whole life.

Surd jokes must step aside for Rajni forwards, parandis must make way for mallipoo, Delhi Daredevils must go down fighting Chennai Super Kings.

Guess what else heads south? Her grades. The princy wants to see more of her parents, her mom wants to see more of kanjivarams and her dad doesn't want to be seen at all. Then there is the school hottie, Tejas, who is making her decidedly hot under the collar. Shiva shiva. How is a girl supposed to cope with all this madness? Read on to find out. Just don't ditch Rinki midway. Mind it!

Read More in Inked

Karma

Cathy Ostlere

An impossible first love,
a girl caught between two worlds,
and a country on the verge of chaos.

Maya never wanted to go to India. She wanted a best friend, a boyfriend, and a mother who wasn't always immersed in grief. Instead, Maya is on a plane from Canada flying halfway around the world with none of those things—only a diary, a pen and an urn.

It's 31 October 1984. Just hours after Maya arrives in Delhi with her father Amar Singh, Prime Minister Indira Gandhi is gunned down by her bodyguards. The assassination sparks riots as Sikh families are killed in retribution. During this chaos Amar disappears and Maya escapes by train to an ancient desert town. She loses her voice but finds a friend in Sandeep, who offers her empathy and bonding in the aftermath of hatred and violence.

A powerful coming-of-age novel, *Karma* is the story of how a young girl facing the demands of two cultures, endures personal tragedy yet learns forgiveness, acceptance and love. Maya and Sandeep invite the reader to look inside their diaries where, in beautiful free verse entries, they reveal an intimate world of secrets, confessions and longings.

Read More in Inked

Cracked

Eliza Crewe

THERE ARE SOME PEOPLE YOU SHOULDN'T ANGER

Ever since my mom was murdered, I've been completely alone. I live in the shadows, because there's no one like me. I have no choice because I have to fight the Hunger, the Hunger that drives me to hunt people and eat their souls. And I have to fight it if I want to stay out of the darkness.

WHO AM I?

I'M MEDA MELANGE.

WHAT AM I?

I DON'T KNOW—BUT I'M NOT HUMAN.

AND NOW, I FINALLY HAVE THE CHANCE TO FIND OUT.

In this gripping novel, find out who Meda is and which side she will come down on, in a thrilling tale of the war between good and evil.